THE SANCTUARY

Tales of Hope and Redemption

THE SANCTUARY

Tales of Hope and Redemption

Krin Van Tatenhove

Cover image: Krin Van Tatenhove via Midjourney and Adobe Firefly

Cover design and interior formatting provided by Casselberry Creative Design.

Story Sanctum Publishing, LLC

ISBN: 979-8-9928559-4-4

Stories are a communal currency of humanity.
- Tahir Shah

Won't you help to sing
These songs of freedom?
'Cause all I ever have
Redemption songs
Redemption songs
- Bob Marley

Dedicated to
Vanessa Desiree (Steward) Davis
1970-2023
Daughter in spirit, imaginary femme,
courageous fighter

Table of Contents

Leaving New Orleans

"This is my favorite part of the trip," said Alberto. We were cruising over the 18-mile span of the Atchafalaya Basin Bridge, en route from San Antonio to New Orleans, windows open to the swamp's humid aroma. Slanting sunlight of a late summer day dappled its surface.

"*Alguna vez hiciste esto cuando eras niño?*" Alberto asked.

I briefly turned my head to see him moving his hand up and down outside his window, mimicking a bird, a plane, or a spacecraft. My Spanish is sketchy, but I understood the gist of his question.

"All the time," I answered. "Especially on long and boring family trips."

Alberto chuckled, a feeble sound, far from his usual resounding laughter, and I was struck again by his decline. He was in the final stages of pancreatic cancer, having survived two chemotherapy regimens. At first, his oncologist objected to our road trip, but she relented when she found out the reason.

"This will likely be his last chance to see him," I told my wife, Lisa. "They've been estranged for a decade and Alberto hopes to make amends."

She shook her head, having never understood my relationship with my older Cuban friend. "Well, I hope it works out for both of them. Just be careful."

I had booked an Airbnb near the French Quarter, close to the pulse of Big Easy nightlife, but I doubted we'd be carousing. Alberto's sole objective was to meet with his only child, Arturo, who had been released from Louisiana's Elayn Hunt Correctional Facility to a halfway house in Metairie. Now in his mid-60s, Arturo had done time for multiple DUIs, the final one resulting in a violent crash that thankfully injured no one but himself. He had recently sent a cryptic message to his father. *I want to see you. There's something I need to say.* Alberto had written scores of letters to Arturo over the years, finally giving up hope of a response. When it arrived so close to his death, he grasped at the chance.

"Do you want to cruise by the halfway house and scout it out before we go to our room?" I asked.

"No, *estoy cansado*. Let's just get a meal and turn in early. I want to be ready for tomorrow."

"As you wish."

Alberto took a sip from his glass of beer, another sign of his condition. He usually drained it in a few gulps.

We were seated in the courtyard of Robert's Gumbo Shop, a block from Jackson Square. Locals and tourists packed the tables around us, and a syncopated Zydeco tune filtered in from the street. Alberto had been silent during our meal, avoiding eye contact. He had a half-eaten po'boy on his plate while I worked on a bowl of crawfish étouffée, nursing my own drink, not wanting to get more intoxicated than him at this delicate phase of his journey.

As I studied him in the light of the patio's outdoor lamps, I thought of how he had always seemed larger than life: six foot two, well-muscled, his olive complexion showing his mixed French and Spanish ancestry. Now, just past his 81st birthday, his pale skin and sunken chest gave witness to his mortal battle.

I reflected on his uniquely American story. At age 18, he left his family and joined the Cuban Exodus that fled to Miami after Castro's victory. There, he lived on the streets until the Cuban Refugee Center, initiated by the Eisenhower Administration, helped him find a job and resettle in Boston. By the time I met him, he was a journeyman electrician. I was visiting some friends in an apartment building and Alberto's balcony was adjacent to theirs. We struck up a conversation and soon discovered that we shared not only an interest in construction skills, but a love of reading and a quirky sense of humor. I later did some odd jobs with him and our relationship began to grow.

Now, he looked up at me with a weak smile. "You remember when I picked you up at the San Antonio airport that first time?"

I grinned and nodded. "How could I forget?"

He had relocated to Texas, and since my prospects had dwindled in Boston, he enticed me with the promise of work. In those days, the Alamo City's airport was small, and you could drive up next to the debarking planes. When I came down the ramp, I saw his vintage Cadillac parked nearby. He had mounted the horns of a steer to the hood and was dressed in a Stetson hat, jeans, chaps, boots, and a frilled western shirt. He looked like the proverbial rhinestone cowboy.

"Howdy pardner," he had said with a fake Texas accent, then moved to embrace me as we laughed from our bellies. We then proceeded to a taqueria for enchiladas and margaritas.

"You have to admit," he said, "I nailed it as a *Tejano vaquero*."

He lifted his drink and tilted it towards me. I did the same and we clinked glasses. Then he grew somber again. I waited, knowing he wanted to share something, but not pushing it, letting his thoughts ripen.

"I keep thinking about those early years," he finally said. "I was such a *pinche* macho asshole. Always pressuring Arturo to be a man, never understanding his quiet nature. Louise constantly told me to go lighter on the kid, but I was my usual stubborn self. She told me he cried himself to sleep for months after I left."

Louise, of Irish-American descent, had married Alberto against her parents' wishes. When their relationship fell apart after a decade, Alberto moved back to Miami for a while, but Louise's strict Catholicism kept her from granting him a legal divorce, so he returned to Boston. Arturo was 10 years old at the time.

"I hear you," I said, "but you know as well as I do, you can't go back and relive those choices."

"Yeah, yeah, but the memories won't leave me alone. And all the drinking I did around him? *Jesucristo!* I remember sitting in my recliner and watching football on Sundays. I would point to Arturo, lift my empty bottle and say, 'beer me up, boy." What an *hijo de puta* I was."

Alberto had always been hard on himself and others. After I joined him in San Antonio, we shared a remodeling business. He could do the work of two men in a single day, and if we had a crew member who slacked off even slightly, Alberto would give him a tongue lashing. His favorite phrase was, "work hard or you'll end up under the bridge." Personally, I loved his style because it aligned with my own high energy and standards. We kicked ass and made a ton of money.

"I've said this before, amigo," I offered, "and I'll say it again. You can't blame yourself for Arturo's alcoholism. If it hadn't been you, someone else would have offered him his first drink. You either have the disease or you don't. It's a form of Russian Roulette that people across our country are playing every day."

"*Claro, pero* it doesn't make me feel any better, no matter how many times you say it."

He pushed his plate away with its half-eaten sandwich and drained the last of his beer. "Let's go back to the room. I want to be as fresh as possible in the morning."

We walked the short distance, Alberto moving slowly and unsteadily, breathing heavily. Then we took turns using the shower. When I came out after mine, he was already asleep on his bed, snoring softly.

I awoke from a vivid dream of lights and laughter on Bourbon Street. Alberto was shaking my shoulder with a vigor I hadn't seen the day before.

"*Levántate, dormilón*," he said. "We've got things to do, places to go."

I roused myself and dressed quickly, noticing the care he had taken with his appearance. He still had a full head of hair, streaked with gray, and he had slicked it back with some sort of gel. He wore a colorful guayabera shirt, dark pants, and a pair of shined shoes. He had neatly trimmed his mustache, but nothing could disguise the pallor of his skin, and his clothes hung a bit limply on his shrinking body.

"Let's go get some java," he said. "Like the last time we were here."

We took the car a few blocks and found a parking spot near Cafe Du Monde. As we sipped our coffee and munched on beignets dusted in powdered sugar, we watched the first stirrings of activity in Jackson Square. A few vendors were setting up on the sidewalks. A musician was tuning his kora, a man I'd heard before, his sounds forever synonymous with New Orleans in my mind. A homeless man was sprawled on the ground beneath the famous statue of Andrew Jackson tipping his hat, the monument's head streaked with lines of pigeon dung. The air smelled of horse manure from the tourist buggies, mixed with stale beer and cigarettes.

"I dreamed about him," said Alberto.

I knew he meant Arturo. "Tell me about it if you're willing."

He shifted his gaze from Jackson Square to me. "He was a boy and we were holding hands, walking on the sands of Playa Pilar in Cuba. The sun was setting and I felt a sense of peace. But then he let go of my hand and began to run ahead of me, and it suddenly got dark. I was afraid he would get lost. It was my duty to find him, but I couldn't see a damn thing."

He placed his hand on his brow, rubbing his forehead.

"It's understandable to feel nervous," I said. "You haven't seen him for so long."

"But why now? After all the letters I sent. And what does he mean by 'there's something I need to say?' Does he want to unload on me one final time? I deserve it but I don't know if could take it."

"Stop borrowing trouble, my friend. Whatever's meant to happen, try to be thankful that you at least get to see him."

He took a deep breath. "*Es la verdad.* If Louise were here, she would say something like 'it's in God's hands.' I never understood that woman's faith."

He checked his watch. "*Vamos.* I want to be early."

We got back in the car and drove to the sober living home in Metairie, about seven miles north. It was in a quiet neighborhood of older houses that needed care but weren't decrepit. I pulled to the curb.

"Do you want me to walk up with you?"

"Do I look like an invalid? Just go and I'll text you

when it's time to pick me up."

I put my hand on his shoulder reassuringly, then he exited the car and walked along a set of large paving stones to the front door. He knocked, the door opened, and after a brief discussion with the person who had answered, he went inside.

With some idle time on my hands, I decided to visit the Metairie Cemetery. I had been there years before on a guided tour, amazed at the elaborate tombs and the stories of illustrious New Orleanians buried there.

I parked in the visitor's lot, then wandered for two hours through the manicured grounds, recognizing many of the sites. The Moorish-style tomb commissioned by Confederate General Beauregard for his beloved daughter Laure; the former resting place of Storyville Madam Josie Arlington, with its bronze figure of a woman knocking at its door; the 60-foot spire marking the graves of Daniel and Mary Moriarty, a final "fuck you" to New Orleans' upper-class who never accepted Moriarty's background as a poor Irish immigrant; the Army of Tennessee tribute to fallen Confederate soldiers, its statue of General Albert Sidney Johnston riding high atop.

I sat on a marble bench in front of a beautiful mausoleum featuring stained glass and wrought iron. I didn't know what the cemetery's smoking regulations were, but since no one was around, I lit a cigarette and sat in the quiet sunlight. Billowing clouds sailed overhead, shifting the shadows of the tombs, like the flickering frames of an old movie.

A memory of Alberto came to mind. He had

supervised the makeover of an expensive home in San Antonio, and its owner took a liking to him, eventually inviting Alberto to attend his daughter's wedding at a posh country club. Alberto was determined to present himself as not just the hired help, but as a man of distinction. He spent a lot of money to rent two tuxedos—a black one for the ceremony, a white one for the reception—changing in the clubhouse locker room. He sent me pictures from his phone that showed him standing in the midst of other guests, clearly overdressed but obviously proud of himself.

I chuckled, took a drag of my smoke, and felt a gentle breeze caress my cheek. It brought the smell of new-mown grass, a reminder that long after the dead dissolve into soil, nature continues its cycles.

I thought about Alberto and Arturo. I knew firsthand that real second chances are rare. My own father and I had never cleared the air between us. I recalled my grief at his funeral, staring down at his body in the casket, thinking of all the things that needed to be said but never would. The recollection still stung after all these years.

But I also treasured the joyful second chance that had happened in my love life. After the failure of my first marriage and the depression that followed it, I despaired of ever finding another partner. Then I met my soul mate, Lisa, and discovered the miracle of unconditional love and support. I was grateful for her every day.

Maybe everything *is* possible, I thought.

I'm not normally a praying man, but I whispered a few words: *If you're listening, God, look favorably on this father and son reunion.*

My phone chirped in my pocket. I pulled it out and saw a text message from Alberto.

I'm done. Come and get me.

I ground my cigarette underfoot, picked up the butt to deposit in a trash can, then turned to retrieve my friend.

———

He was quiet and clearly emotional as we began our return trip. His cheeks quivered as if he was barely holding back his feelings. I noticed a white envelope protruding from the pocket of his shirt. As I had long ago learned with my friend, I stayed silent, letting him decide when or if he wanted to share what had happened.

We had just gotten on the Atchafalaya Basin Bridge going west when he finally spoke.

"Man, I never expected that."

"Expected what?" I asked, noticing with a quick glance that tears were streaming down his pale face.

He swallowed a couple times, trying to collect himself. "I thought he would vent his anger on me. Instead, he asked me to forgive him. Do you hear that? *Me* forgive *him*? *Dios mio!*"

"Forgive him for what?"

"For never taking the time to understand me, even with all my faults. For always blaming me for his mistakes rather than taking personal responsibility. For not seeing that underneath my macho behavior was a man who had always cared for him."

Alberto began to cry softly, a sound that filled the car for a moment. "Then he told me that he loved me."

I was deeply moved, putting my right hand on my friend's shoulder. He reached up his own hand to place it on mine, gently giving me a squeeze. In that touch, I felt all of the bonds we had formed over the years. Then he took that hand and rolled down the passenger window. Once again, the smell of the swamp engulfed us, an odor of verdant life underpinned by decay.

I looked over briefly to see him flying his hand in the air. Up and down, up and down, and then suddenly his arm fell and draped over the windowsill. I knew instinctively what had happened. I knew he was gone. With tears on my cheeks, I drove the final distance to the end of the bridge and found a turnout where I could park.

I got out my phone and called 911 to request an ambulance, then scooted closer to Alberto, feeling for a pulse and finding none. I noticed again the envelope protruding from his pocket. Though it felt like an invasion of privacy, I removed it, opened up the flap, and pulled out a faded Polaroid print. It was Alberto and Arturo when the boy was young, probably just before Alberto moved to Miami. They were standing on the deck of a boat, Boston harbor behind them, holding large fishing poles in their hands and smiling brightly for the camera. At their feet was a string of cod, striped bass, and bluefish, the spoils of their adventure. I flipped the picture over. Scrawled in black ink were the words *A great day together, July 12, 1969*.

I scooted even closer to Alberto, put my arm around him, and tilted his head on my shoulder. Then I waited, the car filled with the whooshing sound of traffic, until I heard a siren in the distance.

I thought again of my Cuban friend in his white tuxedo, his face beaming with pride, recalling a toast he often gave when we shared cervezas.

"Salud, amor, pesetas y tiempo para disfrutarlos!"

I held him tighter and said, "Here's to second chances, mi amigo."

The Buddy System

*A*lways *hike with a buddy, especially in remote areas.* Standard wisdom. He'd heard it since childhood, but Brad ignored it, partially out of necessity. His wife didn't share his passion for mountaineering, and he no longer had friends who enjoyed his strenuous outings. They quickly grew tired of his driven pace, gasping to keep up, irked by his obvious impatience. He knew his refusal to slow down was arrogant, but it was a point of pride in his early 40s, much like others' triathlon victories. He told himself that his solitary style had the benefit of preserving his freedom on the trails. No small talk, just him and the elements as he pushed to bag another summit.

On this day, locked in a swift rhythm, his objective was Wheeler Peak in the Great Basin National Park, towering above the sagebrush flats of Eastern Nevada and Western Utah. It was only a Class 1 hike—just some talus and snow to traverse near the 13,063-foot summit. No need for crampons, ice picks, rope, or pitons. Still, it was steep and rigorous, with guidebooks saying the usual round trip took four to six hours. Brad set a goal of three and a half.

He had parked his truck at the trailhead and started before dawn, wary of forecasts that called for afternoon thunderstorms. His habit when hiking during the summer was to get up and back before any danger. Lightning strikes on hikers were rare, but it happened, and Brad had heard the scorching horror story of a survivor in one of his online forums. Better safe than sorry.

The first section of trail led through meadows and stands of aspens, their leaves winking from green to silver in the sunlight. The peak, carved by ancient glaciers, loomed majestically on the skyline. When he reached Stella Lake, a glacial tarn at 10,400 feet, he stopped for a snack and water.

He took a lungful of thin mountain air and surveyed the rugged landscape. Caddisflies swarmed over the lake, its surface mirroring the granite massif, the blue sky, and a few scuttling clouds. On the opposite shore, a mule deer buck and four does were drinking at the water's edge. It was a living, vibrant painting, on display for anyone who cared enough to find it.

He felt his usual exhilaration, but also another feeling that had grown stronger in recent years. It was a desire to experience the beauty with someone else, a loneliness like a small death settling into his bones. It sapped his vitality and made him feel older.

He took out his phone, snapped a photo, then shook his head and resumed his climb. The trail now took him along the ridgeline. Vegetation gradually disappeared, and the views—extending for hundreds of miles—grew more panoramic with each upwards step. Near the summit, he felt a shift in the weather, a breeze coming down from the heights, tangy with aromas of distant desert, a harbinger of approaching storms. It quickly grew colder, so he paused to remove his parka from his daypack. Then he quickened his pace, determined to add this selfie to his trophy wall.

When he finally reached the top, the vertiginous view was more stunning than he'd imagined, with plummeting descents on all sides. Then he noticed something that made his heart skip. A bank of boiling thunderclouds was approaching, appearing at eye level because of the elevation. Lightning streaked from their blue and black underbellies, thunder rolling over him like shock waves from a distant battle.

Suddenly, he heard a crackling noise in the air, as if a host of locusts surrounded him, and when he looked at his bare arms, he saw the hairs standing on end.

"Shit!" he cried.

Another piece of standard wisdom flashed through his mind. *During a lightning storm, shelter as low as possible, perhaps behind a boulder.* But panic overrode good sense. Pumped on adrenaline, he turned and began to run wildly down the trail, nearly slipping in the shifting rocks, feeling as if an electric entity was trying to swallow him.

Then a loud boom, a crack, and darkness.

"I'm here for you."

A voice drew him back from the shadows. He felt a hand gently shaking his shoulder as he gradually focused on a man's face peering down at him. He looked to be in his forties, wearing a broad-brimmed hat. A chain with two old-fashioned keys hung from his neck. He had a trimmed beard, and his blue-green eyes were filled with concern.

"What happened?" asked Brad, trying to get his bearings.

"A lightning strike knocked you down. Here, let me help you get up."

Brad took the man's extended hand, and as he got shakily to his feet, the man hooked his arm under Brad's shoulder to steady him.

"You're alone up here," said the man. "Not the best decision."

Brad felt irritated despite his grogginess. "I could say the same about you."

The man sighed. "You could. But I'm surrounded by a multitude of friends. Some have even called it a cloud of witnesses."

Brad swung his eyes from side to side, still leaning into the man for support. "I don't see anyone."

"You will."

"What's your name?"

"Call me Pete. And you're Brad."

Brad shook his head in confusion. "How did you know my name?"

"I know a lot of things about you, my impatient, impetuous, driven friend. But right now, buddy, let's get you home."

Lightheaded and faint, Brad leaned more fully against the man, and as he did, he felt a sudden sense of peace and abandon unlike anything he had ever known.

The park ranger spoke into his handheld radio. "His Tacoma is here, just like his wife thought it would be. The entrance sticker is from two days ago. According to her, he would have made this hike much quicker than most people."

The radio crackled. "Better get up the trail and see if you can find him."

"Will do. I'll keep you informed."

The ranger shifted his daypack to a more comfortable position. As he walked alongside the truck towards the trailhead, he looked once again into its vacant interior. He noticed something dangling from the rearview mirror—a chain with two old-fashioned keys. For just a second, it looked like they were glowing.

The ranger rubbed his eyes. *Too much coffee this morning*, he thought, then began his ascent.

What Goes Around...
(dedicated to Tony Morris)

As a man sow, shall he reap. – Bob Marley

You've heard the warning. Don't try this at home. Here's another one for the list. Detoxing from alcohol.

I already knew that, having endured it enough times to prove every theory of alcoholic insanity. But here I was again, 2:00 a.m., alone in bed. My longtime girlfriend, LeAnne, had deserted months earlier, weary of my lurching trip along the bottom. "Don't call me," was her parting salvo, "until you get your act together."

My act was definitely not together. Sweating, nauseous, dehydrated, I tossed and turned, blood pressure hammering my skull. And I was hallucinating, which was a first. Some ancient script kept scrolling across my bedroom ceiling, like words on a teleprompter. I'm fluent in three languages, and I've studied their linguistic histories, but I couldn't decipher a syllable. Even stranger, I kept hearing lyrics from a Tool song, as if a brain worm had crawled out of my ear canal and was taunting me from the darkness: *Why can't we drink forever? I just want to start this over.*

Around four, I got up for water, hungover like a melted corpse in a Dali painting. I tried to orient myself to the date.

Shit, I thought, *it's Thursday morning. I'm going to miss my deadline.*

That deadline was my weekly submission for the newspaper where I worked, one of the great holdouts of print media, a standard in our metropolis for 170 years. People read it during the Civil War, the Oklahoma Land Rush, the dawn of the Industrial Revolution, the two great wars designed to end all wars. They read it through McCarthyism, the Bay of Pigs, the assassination of M.L.K., Jr., the rise of the Internet, the toppling of the World Trade Centers. They were still reading it in print and on their devices.

My only remaining pride was to be part of that grand tradition. A few years earlier, my investigative piece on the dreadful conditions in for-profit prisons had been a finalist for the Pulitzer. I was riding the last fumes of that fame, my disease a riptide pulling me into oblivion.

I stood at the window of my fourth-floor apartment, my reflection as dark and featureless as I felt. A panoramic view of the city spread to the horizon—shimmering lights, bright towers, rivers of red and white traffic. I reached into the top drawer of the dresser, my hand coiling around the grip of a Glock 19. I didn't buy it for home defense. I'd never been to a gun range. It was there for one reason only—to offer a way out if things got too grim.

I lifted it to my head and pressed it above my right ear. As I closed my eyes and tried to suppress my anguish, the only thought I had was, *Call Tony*.

Tony deserved to know that I'd miss my obligation. He was more than my editor. He had been a friend during my descent, encouraging me to get treatment, never threatening to cut me off. My cell phone was on the dresser, so I picked it up and dialed his number. After five rings came a groggy response.

"John...what the hell? Do you know what time it is?"

"I'm sorry," I croaked, my voice dry and hoarse. "I won't be able to get you my article. I'm sorry, Tony."

Silence on the other end.

"Are you okay, John? Do I need to come get you and finally take you for some help?"

"I'm just so tired," I whispered. "I've lost LeAnne. I've lost my pride. And now I can't even meet my deadline. I'm going to make it all go away."

He knew instantly what I meant. "Please don't do that, John. I still believe in you. I believe in your talent. I believe your words have made a difference to so many people. They are *still* making a difference. Your gift will remain and you can start over again."

"I'm tired of starting over. Just so fucking tired. Tired unto death."

Again, a few seconds of silence. My finger tightened ever so slightly on the trigger.

"John, I'm pleading with you. Get up off your knees and try again, this time in a new way. Let me pick you up and take you somewhere for treatment."

I stood there, frozen, staring out at the city, my hand cocked to my head, as tears began to roll down my cheeks.

Two years later

In the break room that day, a colleague asked me, "What's the greatest lesson you've learned in sobriety?" I don't think he was really interested, just being polite. Non-alcoholics are muggles when it comes to understanding the disease. It was hard to choose an answer, but I used an adage from my Twelve Step meetings. Accepting life on life's terms. A humble acknowledgment that there's so much we can't control. Or, to put it another way, there's so much we should *never even try to control*. Control is an addiction all its own. My colleague nodded, then said, "Well, I admire you, John."

I leaned back in my desk chair and thought of how that answer stemmed from multiple hard lessons. Since that fateful morning when Tony drove me to rehab, I'd gotten ample opportunities to practice letting go. I had called LeAnne, but she had no desire to reunite, having found someone who, she said, "was more stable." Then there was the newspaper continuing its transition to an online presence, hiring freelancers and paying them a pittance. My salary was downsized. Tony and I met for coffee once a week, and he tried to explain it as my friend, but I didn't blame him. It was the new reality, and he was even questioning the security of his own position.

To make ends meet, I'd taken a job as an adjunct

professor at a local junior college, teaching courses online. It was mildly enjoyable but never fulfilling. I longed for those years when I was hot on the trail of an investigative project, tracking it down and bringing it into focus. That was my passion, my highest calling, and I was afraid my newfound acceptance would turn into toxic regret.

Then, at one of our weekly confabs, Tony surprised me.

"I have some news, John. I got a call from a midsize paper in the Midwest. Instead of surrendering, they want to try and resurrect their presence. They offered me a job as Editor-in-Chief, hoping I can turn things around."

Since Tony was my only real friend, my first thought was *Here we go again, another thing to accept.* But I pushed that aside. "Are you going to take it?"

In his mid-50s, twenty years my senior, Tony still dressed like a hipster. Graphic T-shirts from rock concerts, a leather jacket, pressed chinos, thick-framed glasses of various colors, and one of the many fedoras he collected. He took off his hat, running his hand through his goatee, then over his bald head. I'd seen him do it a thousand times.

"Yeah. I already signed a contract. I would have told you sooner but the negotiations were touch and go."

He took a sip of coffee. "It was hard to convince Joanne, but both of us have fantasized about living in a smaller city with less congestion. Plus, my job here isn't stable."

I nodded, trying to hide my disappointment. "I'm happy for you. You deserve only the best. Both you and Joanne."

"Thanks, but there's more. The paper gave me the latitude to bring in new talent. I'd like to offer you a job as my top journalist."

Looking back on that moment, there was a shift in me. I'd heard countless people describe their beliefs that some higher power, some God or force, was accomplishing in their lives what they could not do for themselves. It was that instant when I made a baby step towards believing. It was like a puzzle piece snapping into place. I had no prospects, only my wistfulness about the past, and I, too, had grown tired of the impersonal vibes of the city.

"Let me think about it, Tony," I said, but I knew in my heart that I was ready.

Summer, two years later

I shut down my computer, pleased with my latest installment in a series on fentanyl trafficking in the Midwest. It featured three families whose lives had been tragically damaged by the substance and were speaking out to make a difference. It wasn't easy reading, but it was timely and prophetic. The narrative arcs were strong. I was feeling my old mojo.

I looked out the window of my office. The building that housed the newspaper was on the edge of town, bordered by a sweeping expanse of corn fields, the cash crop of the Midwest. Accustomed to urban landscapes, I was surprised by how much I had grown to love the vastness and tranquility of my new home. Sometimes I'd get in my car and drive to the middle of nowhere, clearing my head. Or sit at a roadside picnic table and practice letting my past and present converge into a sense of serenity.

My thoughts turned to Tony. He had overseen great progress at the paper, but I was worried about him. Joanne's reluctance to move had blossomed into discontent. She said she missed the cultural opportunities of the big city and complained that their new neighbors were parochial. Finally, she left Tony with an ultimatum that if he didn't join her within a year, their marriage was over. That deadline had come and gone.

Simultaneously, Tony developed back problems— aggravated by stress and too many hours at a desk. He underwent surgery to fuse three lower vertebrae, and the pain meds they gave him during recovery got their talons into him. He had lost some of his sharpness. I saw it. So did others. It was the proverbial elephant in the newsroom. When I expressed my concern, he thanked me, shifting his gaze to the side, then told me everything would be okay, yet I knew firsthand how addicts minimize their usage.

The irony struck me—my own addiction and denial, his support as a friend, even the fact that I was investigating opioid trafficking. I wanted to help him, and I felt poised to make a difference in his life, but people only change when they're ready.

On this day, he had phoned in sick. It had happened other times recently, and the staff was getting more suspicious. I waited until late afternoon, then called him. No answer. I waited until nightfall and tried again. Still no answer. Highly unusual.

I decided to drive to his house for a welfare check. He lived on the edge of town near a creek bed bordered by tall trees and a hiking trail. The stream was damned in various spots to create ponds where people could sit and absorb the scenery.

I parked next to his car in the driveway and got out. The streetlights were on, already attracting swarms of bugs. It was a warm summer night and I could smell the creek bottom, damp and mossy. When I got to the front door, it was slightly ajar, stoking my worries. I pushed it open.

"Tony," I called out. "Are you here? It's John. I'm just checking on you."

No answer. I entered and made a quick search of the modest home, noting the decorations that showed Joanne's sense of style. He wasn't there. I thought about calling the police; maybe there'd been foul play. But I also knew that Tony liked to hike along the creek to a favorite spot near one of the ponds. I would check there before calling the authorities.

The paved trail along the water had light poles spaced at intervals, but it was still gloomy. Frogs and crickets had begun their evening symphony, accompanied by the gurgling of the creek. I quickened my stride and, sure enough, as I approached the first pond I could see Tony's unmistakable form, his bald head reflecting light from a pole just above him. He was seated on a bench, and when I slid next to him, he looked at me.

I'll never forget his eyes. They mirrored my own that night I had pressed the gun against my temple. It was the gaze of a man trapped in his personal purgatory, conceding the doom of a repetitive behavior that would grind him throughout eternity.

He tried hard to focus. "John? What are you doing

here?" His voice was soft and raspy.

"I'm here to help you, Tony. I know the pills have taken you down. I know that Joanne leaving is still depressing you."

He turned away, his breathing labored. The plaintive call of a lonesome owl drifted out of the darkness.

"Too much," he whispered. "Just too much."

"I know," I said, "But I want to remind you of some words you said to me a couple years ago. I believe in you, Tony. I believe in your talents. I believe in how you care for other people. Hell, I wouldn't be sitting her next to you unless you had stayed by me."

He began to shake, a tremor running through his body. Then he slumped forward, placing his arms on his legs. One of them slipped and I was afraid he would topple over, so I supported him under his armpit.

"Come with me, my friend. Let's get you the help you need."

He rubbed his right hand over his head and sighed. "Okay, John. Okay."

A year later

The hotel's grand ballroom, with its opulent chandeliers and art deco design, was a splendid choice for our region's journalistic awards banquet. The tables sported newsprint tablecloths, and large TVs on the walls displayed the year's best photos and art.

Our staff had carpooled to the capital, an annual trek that we all enjoyed. Seated at our table, my colleagues were drinking wine or cocktails from the open bar as I nursed a ginger ale. Tony sat next to me, sipping a Diet Coke. As I looked around at their faces, I thought of how far afield our life's paths can take us. We end up in divergent realities we never expected, but when we make them our own, they enrich us immensely.

Just moments before, I had received an award for my series on fentanyl. A far cry from contending for the Pulitzer, but somehow more valuable to me given all that had happened in the past few years. As the evening neared its climax, they were about to announce the ultimate award—Journalist of the Year.

The MC, Editor-in-Chief of the state's largest newspaper, went to the microphone.

"Ladies and gentlemen," she said, "thank you for being here. Let me congratulate all those who have received awards this evening. We are a talented group. Together, we're keeping journalistic excellence alive in a rapidly changing world of sound bites and short attention spans."

She lifted her glass. "A toast to our continued success in the coming year."

There was a raucous chorus of "Here! Here!" that died down in anticipation of her announcement.

"And now," she continued, "we come to tonight's most prestigious award. I would ask for the envelope, but there isn't one."

The crowd tittered.

"With no further ado, let me recognize our journalist of the year, Tony Harris, for your editorial prowess, your sharp wit, and your business acumen."

The room exploded with applause, and people began

to shout, "Speech! Speech!"

Tony looked genuinely surprised. He got up and made his way steadily to the podium, evidence that his physical therapy was making a difference. He took the mic from the MC, then ran his hand through his goatee and over his head before scanning the room in a moment of silence. Everyone quieted down.

"For those of us who have ink in our blood," he said, "this night is a celebration of that passion that will not let us go. And I can't thank you enough for this honor."

He looked down for a moment, clearly emotional.

"I want to share a truth that I've learned firsthand. Karma can be a bitch, but it can also be the force that saves our lives. I won't get into the details of how deeply I understand this, but I just want to say one other thing."

He'd taken his Coke with him to the front.

"I have a personal toast to my friend for many years, John Newcombe."

He lifted his glass.

"John, what goes around comes around. You know what I mean, brother, and I'm eternally grateful for our relationship."

Tears welled in my eyes. I lifted my tumbler and toasted not only to Tony, but to every suffering soul, every individual trapped in purgatory, every person teetering on the edge of a decision that was as final as the closing of a coffin lid. And for every last one of them, I poured out a silent prayer of hope and healing.

"Here! Here!" shouted the crowd around me.

El Padrino

We must learn to regard people less in the light of what they do or omit to do, and more in the light of what they suffer. – Dietrich Bonhoeffer

December 2010, near the Mexican/American border

*I*t was early morning, the cold winter air tinged with smoke from trash fires. Our crew of volunteers was inspecting construction sites in a colonia on the outskirts of Reynosa, Mexico. The neighborhood was mostly shacks cobbled together from old wood, tin, and cardboard. No running water or electricity. Many of its residents were migrants from Chiapas, lured to jobs in maquiladoras along the border. They weren't squatters. They had purchased their tiny lots with a mortgage and now were laboring with us to build 500 square-foot, cement block structures with two bedrooms and a living space that included a kitchen.

Latrines remained outside. These modest homes would usually shelter large families.

I was looking forward to a day of laboring alongside new homeowners, a fellowship of shared purpose, but first I was called elsewhere. News had rippled through the dirt streets that a pastor was present, and I'd received an invitation from a family to bless their newborn child.

I was willing, even though I knew my words would be a clumsy mixture of English and Spanish. A member of the community guided me to the family's shelter, a one-room shack for two adults and three children. Its walls were scrap plywood, its roof rusted tin over a floor of barren earth. Outside was a cooking fire and a pit latrine.

An old bench seat from a bus sat near the entrance, listing slightly, its surface torn to reveal the springs beneath. The parents, Oscar and Claudia Salazar, thanked me for coming and asked me to sit. Then they brought their tiny daughter to me, only three weeks old.

"Que preciosa," I said. "Come se llama ella?"

"Perla," was the answer.

I cradled the infant in my arms, bundled in a blanket. She was quiet, her dark eyes staring up at me, and though I knew she would never remember that moment, it was sacramental for me.

I made the sign of the cross on her forehead and prayed for our Creator's guiding hand to be upon her and her family, giving them strength, safety, and abundance for this new life they sought to establish.

Then I held her against my chest for a moment, encircled by her family and smiling neighbors. I could hear dogs barking in the distance.

July 2025, San Antonio, Texas

It was mid-morning. I was sitting in my office when my phone buzzed. I didn't recognize the number.

"This is Alex," I answered.

"Alex, it's Peter Banks. It's been a while, amigo."

Peter's nonprofit had organized the housing projects in Reynosa, partnering with Habitat Para la Humanidad. I knew that the rise of violence with the Gulf Cartel had forced him to shift his focus to immigration advocacy in the U.S. Meanwhile, I'd left my life as a cleric a decade earlier. When people asked me why, I told them it wasn't due to a crisis of faith. It was an expansion of faith that could no longer be contained by organized religion. I now worked for a nonprofit that oversaw grants for people living with disabilities.

"What's it been?" I said. "Eight or nine years?"

"That sounds about right."

"Good to hear from you, Peter. To what do I owe the pleasure?"

"Do you remember the Salazar family?"

The memory of that day returned, as well as its aftermath. The Salazars had sent a picture to me a year later. They were standing in front of their cement block home, Perla supported by her mother's hand. The photo was in an envelope scrawled with the words "Al Padrino de Perla." *Godfather?* I thought. I was a bit embarrassed that my momentary gesture could be held in such high esteem. I felt unworthy.

"How could I forget?"

"Well, you won't believe this, but they're here in the city. They found a way to enter illegally and they've sought refuge and help from our center."

"All five of them?"

"No, just Perla and her parents. Her older brothers struck out on their own. One lives in Matamoros, the other in Monterrey."

Immediately, the danger of their situation was clear. Our city, like so many in the US, had ICE agents raiding businesses, homes, and public parks, arresting people without legal papers and transporting them to detention centers.

"I'm confused," I said. "The last time I heard from them, they had a built a small home. Why did they leave?"

"I think it would be better if you heard from them firsthand. Could you come to our offices by the back door this afternoon? There's some urgency here."

We set a time for 4:00 p.m.

The room Peter chose for our meeting was tucked in the back of his headquarters, one of three homes his operation used on our city's impoverished South Side. The window blinds were drawn tight. Claudia and Oscar Salazar sat on a couch with Perla beside them. The parents rose and greeted me with warm hugs, as if we were long lost relatives. Perla remained seated, watching me with a distant expression. She was now 15, but she looked older, an attractive young woman with a touch of hardness about her. I nodded at her and smiled, but she simply held my eyes with a flat stare.

"Let's get started," said Peter, turning to Oscar. "Por favor, cuéntale a Alex la historia de por qué estás aquí."

"Claro," said Oscar, fixing his eyes on mine and beginning his explanation in rapid Spanish.

I caught most of it and Peter translated the rest. It was painful to hear. Claudia and Oscar had secured jobs at the LG Electronics factory in Reynosa, assembling TVs for international distribution. They staggered their shifts so that one of them could always be home to watch over the three children. When the boys moved out, Perla began to associate with peers that had a negative influence on her. She hooked up with a boyfriend who had ties to Los Metros, a faction of the Gulf Cartel that controls northern cities in the Mexican state of Tamaulipas. He became possessive, then physically abusive, and when she tried to pull away, he threatened her and her family. Oscar and Claudia hoped it would simmer down over time, but it grew worse. Twice during the night, their home was struck with rocks, and guns were fired over their roof.

"Dios mío," I said. "Did you go to the police?"

Clauda and Oscar smiled tolerantly, and Perla made a scoffing noise, speaking up for the first time.

"The police are corrupt. If we went to them for help, it would only have made things worse."

I was surprised by her English fluency, arching my eyebrows.

"The Salazars paid for an ESL tutor at Perla's request," Peter explained. "On both sides of the border, being bilingual opens a lot of doors."

I nodded and looked at her. "I admire that. Can you tell me what happened next?"

She continued in English that was a bit stilted but understandable. She said their family had a cousin in Houston who had emigrated many years ago. He secured his citizenship and now ran a string of small businesses in the Second Ward, a strong Latino enclave. The Salazars pleaded for his help. Even though human smuggling was mostly controlled by the cartel, he knew a man who drove an independent produce truck between Reynosa and McAllen, Texas. He had designed a hidden chamber in the flatbed, and with so many pallets of produce stacked on top, he had never had border agents discover it. For a steep price, he could get them across.

"I have never been so scared," said Perla. "Not even when Los Metros attacked our home. We were lying flat on our backs. It was so dark. I could hear traffic and the inspectors speaking to the driver. I thought they would find us. I thought they would arrest us and take us to a Centro de Detención."

I could hear the fear in her voice. My heart went out to them, confirming a truth that is central to my life. No matter how different someone's experience is from ours, when we enter into their stories, we have a chance to practice love and hospitality.

"We have a couple drivers who transport people from the border to San Antonio," said Peter, "but no one available to get them to Houston. Is there any chance you could help, Alex?"

I looked at the expectant faces of the Salazars. Even

Perla's expression was now softer.

"Of course," I said. "They can come home with me now and we'll leave early in the morning. I'll take a personal day."

"Gloria a Dios," said Claudia, tears streaming down her cheeks.

I had made a snap decision without consulting my wife, Yasmin, but her reaction didn't surprise me. A second generation Mexican American, she managed a gallery at a local arts complex that specialized in exhibits of Latinx artists. Politically, she was further left than I am. At her insistence, we'd just attended a protest against the ICE raids that were rampant since the new administration took office. The experience moved me deeply. We chanted and sang with a crowd of thousands, and Yasmin described the vibe of the crowd as *el Espiritu Santo del pueblo.*

Yasmin greeted the Salazars with open arms and helped them get settled, using our guest bedroom and a pull-out sofa bed in the living room. Our two daughters were away at college, so we had ample room. Then the five of us shared a simple dinner. Fluent in Spanish, Yasmin engaged the Salazars, drawing out more of their story. What struck me was the bravery of these parents who had left everything behind at great risk to protect their only daughter.

I told the Salazars that we would leave before dawn, then we all went to our rooms to get rested for the trip.

At 2:10 a.m., I heard loud knocking on our front door. Expecting the worst, I got up and went to the entrance. It was wise to have home security in our neighborhood, and because I'm a bit of a techie, I had installed a larger than normal screen near the door. It showed a view all the way to the street. Perla stirred from the nearby sofa bed, but I gestured with my hand for her to stay back.

Three ICE agents were standing in the glow of our porch light, one slightly in front of the others. They were dressed in black with bullet proof vests. Pistols, radios, and handcuffs hung from their utility belts. Emblazoned on their chests in white block letters were the words ICE POLICE. They wore dark masks.

"I know you can see us," said the man in front. "We have reason to believe that you are sheltering illegal immigrants. Open the door."

My anxiety was replaced by a growing anger, especially at their anonymity.

"Do you have a warrant?" I asked.

"No," said the leader, "but it would be wise for you to cooperate."

"I'm not letting you in my house without a warrant."

The leader turned and whispered something to his comrades that I couldn't decipher. Then he turned back to me.

"I must insist that you open the door."

"You can insist all you want, but without a warrant I will not let you in my home."

He snorted in frustration, letting his hand drop to his gun. It only pissed me off further.

"And while you're standing there," I said, "why don't you take off your mask? What's the matter? Afraid to let me see your face?"

He stood frozen for a moment, then reached up and removed it. He was young, Latino, with a beard and dark eyes.

"There. Satisfied?"

I looked into his eyes and the same truth I had applied to the Salazars filled my mind. Who was this young man who had once suckled at his mother's breast? What was his story? What were his hopes, his dreams, the challenges he faced?

"Well, fellow American," I said, "we may be on opposite sides of this door, but we aren't enemies. We share the same country and the same constitutional rights. Without a warrant, I won't let you past my threshold."

He just shook his head. "This isn't over, sir. Not by a long shot." Then he turned and the three of them walked out to the street and vanished.

I let out a deep breath, realizing only then how much adrenaline was coursing through me. Yasmin and the Salazars had gathered in the hallway, listening to the discussion.

Yasmin came up behind me and placed her hand on my shoulder. "My husband," she said, "thank you for that. I have an idea for what to do next."

———

A few hours later, we implemented Yasmin's plan. Since she and I both drive SUVs, she suggested that she leave our garage into the rear alleyway before dawn, using my vehicle with its darker window tinting. If we were under surveillance, perhaps she could act as a decoy. A short time later, I could leave in her car with the Salazars. It was still risky, but it was the best shot we had.

Yasmin left at 5:00 a.m. A half hour later, I loaded the Salazars into Yasmin's car. It has three back seats, so I instructed them to lie down, one to a seat, until we were clear of the city.

I pulled out and made my way to Interstate 10 for our three-hour drive to Houston. I was only nervous now, no anger, and I obsessively checked the rearview mirrors to see if we were being followed. It wasn't until we got past Seguin that I began to relax, telling the Salazars they could sit up in their seats.

Perla was right behind me, staring at me through the rearview mirror. I looked into her eyes, remembering that distant day when I held her on a broken bus bench, the smell of smoke surrounding us.

"Gracias, padrino," she said.

"Es mi privilegio."

And we smiles at each other as we hurtled towards the next chapter of her life.

Robbed on Credit

Costa Grande, Mexico, 1983

When I think about that day that changed my life, I remember the plane descending into Acapulco. White clouds drifted over the green Sierra Madres sloping to the sea, and I saw colorful tourist umbrellas on the beach. I would rent a car at the airport, then drive north to Zihuatanejo—Zihua to locals—a growing destination along the coast.

Dad moved there when I was 28. He had visited for years, even buying a hillside lot in the mid-70s before Mexico poured 50 billion pesos into the area to promote tourism. Once he migrated, I wondered if I would see him again, but he periodically called me to fly south and help with his "projects." One time, it was clearing the land where he planned to build his house. Another time, we remodeled a studio he leased in town. He covered my expenses and we shared the room he rented. He could have easily found local labor, but I knew he wanted to see me, and I appreciated it. On this trip we would paint the exterior of his new home.

Neither of us imagined the shocking evening ahead of us.

Born of Mexican parents on the US side of the border, Dad met Mom in San Diego. Her heritage was Dutch, and her parents taught in local school districts. She followed in their footsteps while Dad struggled as an artist. They never married, separating after seven years, but they claimed that my birth was one of the best things that happened in their lives. With Mom, I felt the truth of that sentiment. With Dad, not so much.

He was a man of extremes, flashing intense anger if he saw an injustice, laughing loudly at something he found funny, or withdrawing into a remote silence. I never knew what to expect and I always felt off balance around him. Most of all, I sensed that his inner life was vastly different than what he projected. I saw the evidence in his wildly eclectic paintings. Some were surreal depictions of Mayan symbols and temples. Others were serene landscapes of the Costa Grande, the water so vibrant you felt it would pour off the canvas. At other times, he turned to portraiture, bringing *campesinos* to life in an almost photographic way.

Who was the man beneath the exterior? My mother told me she could never reach his core. I grew up feeling the same thing, and his inaccessibility left a vacancy in my life, especially since he wasn't physically affectionate. I once heard a psychologist say that a young man needs to send his taproot into the aquifer of his father's love. My root never found that reservoir.

As the plane's tires jolted on the tarmac that fateful morning, I realized again what I hated to admit to myself in my mid-30s.

At some level, I still craved Dad's approval.

Dad and I drank beer as we stood under an awning in front of his cement block home. It was a modest structure with a bedroom, kitchen, and small living area, purified water supplied through a refillable tank on the roof. The toilet was outside and worked on a septic system. Perched halfway up a hill, it had a panoramic outlook on Zihua Bay.

"I know my digs aren't much," said Dad, "but you gotta love the million-dollar view."

I chuckled, "No one would argue with that."

"How's your mother doing? How often to you see her?"

"A couple times a month. She told me to tell you hi and that she wishes you well."

He shook his head slowly, then took another swig of beer. "Yeah? Well, tell her I said the same thing."

The sun was setting over the Pacific, a smoldering ball of reddish orange that seemed reticent to abandon the day. It illuminated the water with an otherworldly glow, like a psychedelic album cover by Roger Dean. I looked at Dad's rugged features, profiled in the fading light, a man my mother said had melted her heart, reshaped it, melted it again, then finally left it numb and indifferent. "How's the painting going?"

"My mojo comes and goes, but mostly I'm pleased. I'm selling more pieces to the tourists who are discovering Zihua. What about you? How's that new job?"

I had recently accepted a position at a junior college in Southern California, teaching computer science in the days when IBM had just released its 386 PC and the launching of the Internet was still five years away.

"I really like it. It's a growing field and I love having to keep pace with the emerging technology."

He nodded, then we stood in silence as twilight deepened along the steep dirt road that led to town. Dad reached behind him and pulled the string for a lone outdoor bulb, creating an umbrella of yellow light around us.

Suddenly, a commotion arose from down the hill— shouting, dogs barking, then the unmistakable crack of a gunshot. It grew louder until three men emerged from the shadows. As they got closer, I could see they were dressed in police uniforms, their guns in hand. (Note: even though Dad and I are bilingual, I'm sharing this primarily in English. I want my friends in America to understand what these events meant to me).

One of the men walked boldly towards Dad, brandishing his pistol. "You're under arrest, gringo!"

"Why?" Dad's voice was surprisingly calm.

"*Porque?*" said the leader, his smirk visible in the dim light. "We don't need to tell you that until we get you to the station. Is that what you want, *cabrón?*"

There was something off about these men. They didn't fill out their uniforms with the usual robust physiques of *policia*. They were greasy and unshaven, and when I looked at the other two who stood behind the leader, their eyes shifted away. The smell of stale alcohol and sweat rolled off them like fumes from a dumpster.

"I've done nothing," Dad said. "Leave me and my son alone."

The leader stepped closer, pressing his gun against Dad's chest, then pulling it back. My heart flopped like a fish on a deck, and my mouth went dry.

"I have a better idea. Give us your money. We know you have some. We've watched you do business at your art gallery. Give us your money and we'll walk away."

"I don't have any money here."

Dad's voice was softer now, more tentative, but his words threw a match into this combustible mix of thievery. The other two men surged forward. They began to beat Dad, slugging him in the chest, kicking his legs. One of them threw a roundhouse punch that caught Dad on the jaw and brought him to his knees.

The leader had stepped back, but now he walked over to me, lifted his gun and shot a round into the dirt at my feet. The explosion stung my ears.

"Have you seen the old movies in your United States?" he said with a laugh. "The ones where the ridiculous Mexican *bandido* shoots the ground and yells, 'Dance gringo, dance!'"

He laughed even louder, then lifted his pistol over his head and shot another round into the air.

"OK," gasped Dad. "*Bastante.* I'll take you to the money, but we need to walk up the hill to get it."

The leader was instantly suspicious. "Up the hill?

I don't believe you. *Está en tu casa.* Don't try to trick us, gringo."

"Why would I do that?" said Dad. "You have the guns. I keep it buried up the hill, but I can take you there."

It was a pivotal moment. The three men looked at each other, conveying messages in their glances as one of them shrugged. Then they turned their eyes back to us.

"We will give you a few moments," said the leader, "but you better not be lying or you will not like what happens to you and your son."

Dad regained some of his composure. "*Entiendo.* I need to grab some flashlights and a shovel first."

"Do it," commanded the leader.

Dad got up painfully from the ground and walked to a small wooden lean-to at the side of the house. One of the henchmen followed closely, his gun leveled at Dad's back. A few moments later they returned with two large flashlights and a sturdy shovel.

"This way," said Dad, pointing to a path that ran around the side of the house and ascended through the trees behind it.

The leader snatched one of the flashlights from Dad and handed it to me. Then he pointed his gun at me and tilted his head towards Dad. "You go with your father in front. *Escúchame!* Don't try anything stupid."

I felt drugged by a cocktail of fear and adrenaline, but I nodded and joined Dad as we circled the house and began climbing. I looked at him as he turned his head slightly and winked at me.

A wink? What the hell did *that* mean? I couldn't

ever remember Dad winking. Was he saying I should trust him? Did it mean he had some chicanery planned that might put us both in danger? Again, I felt that vertigo of not understanding him, nervous at his unpredictability.

The path up the hill was tricky with only two small shafts of light guiding us. The gravelly dirt was slippery and I almost lost my footing a couple of times. I could hear the men breathing heavily behind us and could smell their pungent body odor.

We hiked about 50 yards before Dad suddenly stopped. "This is the spot."

Here?" said the leader, still suspicious. "Why here? I don't believe you."

"You will in a moment."

"Then dig, gringo!"

I illuminated the ground as Dad took his shovel and began to overturn the packed earth. Honestly, I had to agree with the leader. Why here? There was no rock or piece of wood to serve as a marker. What was Dad up to?

After a few moments, longer than any of us expected, the leader growled. "You lied to us, you dog. Now you will pay the price!"

Suddenly, the shovel hit something with a clang. Dad reached into the hole and pulled out a medium-sized metal box. The leader snatched it from his grasp, quickly sprung the latch, then began to rifle through the contents. Papers that looked official fell to the ground, as well as some Polaroid photographs. The leader pulled out a roll of bills secured with a rubber band. I could see they were American dollars, not pesos. He peeled through them, counting.

"This is it?" he shouted, nearly spitting in Dad's face. "You bring us all the way up for this? I knew you were lying! You will need to bury your dead!"

As if on cue, the other two men stepped forward and began to beat Dad again until he fell to his knees. That's when I saw Dad reach beneath his shirt and pull out a pendant that hung from a leather strap around his neck. He held it up, an amulet made of obsidian with a crystal imbedded in it. It sparkled in the glow from my flashlight.

Dad pushed himself away from the two men attacking him, lifted the amulet with one hand and said in a raspy voice, "Doña Maria, *ayudame!*"

The robbers froze as if someone had stopped a projector. Dad could see that he had gotten their attention.

"It is the three of you who will have to bury your dead," he said, his voice growing stronger, "because I am under the protection of Doña Maria."

I had heard Dad talk about her. She was an old woman who lived on the upper floor of a small curio shop in town. The locals believed she was a witch, a *bruja*, who could curse people with her magic. Dad didn't ascribe to that superstition. She was a healer, he said, a *curandero*, and he sometimes sought her out for spiritual advice. But she allowed the negative gossip to persist, a way to secure protection for a woman living alone.

Dad stood taller, snatched the flashlight from my hand, and swept its beam across the faces of the three robbers. There was now an obvious fear in their eyes which emboldened Dad. He took the offense, stepping towards them, still holding the amulet in front of him.

"If you had needed some money, why didn't you just come to me and ask for help?"

Two of the men looked at the ground, shuffling their feet. The leader made a half-hearted scoffing sound.

"Where do you live?" said Dad.

"Why would we tell you that?" asked the leader. "So the *bruja* can put a curse on us?"

"No," said Dad, "so that I can bring you the rest of your money in the morning."

What the hell? Why was Dad making false promises? Who in their right mind would believe such a statement?

"You're crazy, gringo," said the leader. "Others in town say that about you. The man who paints the strange visions. I won't tell you where we live."

Dad extended the amulet even further towards the leader. "Then Doña Maria will certainly hear about what you have done tonight."

The leader looked to the ground, shook his head, then muttered an address.

"I know that *colonia*," said Dad. "Go. I will bring you more money tomorrow. And don't *ever* come near my home again. Don't *ever* threaten me or my son again. *Comprendes*?"

The leader's shoulder slumped. He nodded, then turned and motioned his men to follow him down the hill, where their silhouettes quickly dissolved in the darkness.

Once they were gone, Dad doubled over in pain.

"Help me get back to the house," he muttered.

The way down was harder, holding a flashlight in my right hand and supporting Dad on my left shoulder. As we shuffled through the dirt, I thought again of his wink. Had the amulet been part of his plan the whole time? If so, why hadn't he shown it earlier? Nothing made sense except that we had escaped possible death. I could feel my adrenaline beginning to subside.

When we got to his porch, he unwrapped from me and leaned against the house in that yellowish glow from the bulb. He looked squarely at me, a huge bruise forming on his jaw where he'd been sucker-punched.

"Dad," I said, "why did you promise them you'd go there in the morning? You're not really thinking..."

My words were interrupted as he suddenly moved towards me and took me in his arms.

How can I describe that moment? I thought it would be brief, and I admit I was stiff, so unaccustomed to any affection. But he held me firmly until I relaxed into the warmth of his embrace. I don't know how long we stood there, but I could hear him softly crying, and in those moments I felt the reservoir of his love flood into me.

The sun had barely risen the next morning when Dad came to my room.

"I have that business to deal with," he said. "I'd like you to come with me, but it's your choice."

The bruise on his jaw had turned purple overnight, and there was a jagged scratch across his forehead. I suddenly felt protective of him like I never had before. Since there seemed to be no stopping his crazy scheme, I said, "Of course I'll come."

Dad knew Zihua intimately. We walked down the hill, with him obviously in pain, until he hailed a dilapidated taxi, its driver a grizzled older man with a stubble of gray beard. An icon of La Virgen de Guadalupe hung from his rearview mirror. Dad directed him first to a local bank, where he withdrew money from an ATM. Then he gave the address we had heard the night before from the leader.

"Are you sure you want to go there?" asked the driver. "It is not the safest place for gringos."

I was wondering the same thing, a knot of fear forming in my stomach. Though I'd agreed to go on this errand, I connected again with those feelings of uncertainty about Dad and his motives. Were we about to relive last night's drama? Was he placing us in danger again?

"*Estoy seguro*," said Dad.

We drove on the main road out of town, along the Malecon and the beaches, the Pacific on our right dappled with morning sunshine, passing hotels and condos under construction. A squadron of pelicans flew near us with tight precision. When we reached the outskirts, the driver turned up a slight hill into a section of shanties, winding his way expertly along twisting dirt streets until we came to a what I can only describe as a hovel—unfinished cement block patched with drywall and plywood, corrugated tin for a roof. A mangy dog from a nearby shack started yapping at our arrival, and two malnourished pigs were snuffling and nosing in the dirt. The air smelled of smoke and garbage, tinged with ocean brine carried on an inland breeze.

After instructing the driver to wait, Dad turned to me. "You stay here."

"No way. I'm not letting you face this alone."

Dad smiled, almost sadly. "Then stay back a bit. Promise?"

I nodded as we got out of the taxi. Dad limped across the dirt yard to a plywood door and knocked. No one answered. He tried again more forcefully. Finally, it opened and I could see it was the leader. He was barefoot, wearing old jeans and a wrinkled version of the cop's shirt from the night before, this time open to reveal a stained tank top with a Corona beer ad. A small boy clad only in diapers peered out from between his legs.

He looked at Dad with surprise, then down at the dirt, then back up again, slowly shaking his head. The two of them exchanged a few words which I couldn't hear clearly. Then Dad handed him the envelope with the money and turned on his heels. The leader watched for a second, still shaking his head, then closed the door.

As Dad got nearer to me, he straightened to his full height, squared his shoulders, and pulled out the amulet from around his neck. He kissed it, then slid it back beneath his shirt, turning his gaze to me with that slightly sad smile.

In that moment, something in my heart changed forever. Dad seemed larger than life, capable of more compassion than I'd ever imagined. Even capable of showing mercy towards those who had harmed him, a love for one's enemies that many a Christian mouthed as a platitude but rarely practiced. I saw the core of this man and I loved him beyond measure.

He stopped a few feet from me and wiggled his eyebrows like an imitation of Groucho Marx. "Well, I hope that's the first and last time I ever get robbed on credit."

Then he winked and we burst into laughter as the taxi driver honked his horn impatiently behind us.

The Wedding Night Tape

Pomona, California, June 25th, 1985

The Los Angeles Basin sweltered under summer sun, and the eye-watering smog, pushed inland by Pacific breezes, banked like fog against the San Bernardino Mountains. It was miserable.

I was on my last stop in one of Pomona's trailer parks, a pocket of poverty in a city renowned for its gang activity. My job was simple. After the deregulation of the cable industry in 1984, start-up companies seized the opportunity. Mine supplied me with addresses of homes that had no cable. We offered 6 months free, secured by a small deposit, hoping that by padding our database of clients, we could eventually sell out to a larger competitor. My uncle was the company founder, so even though I was an entry-level grunt trying to prove myself, I had aspirations for a cut of future profits.

I wiped my sweaty forehead as I approached a mobile home that was old but in good condition. Its front porch extended the length of the trailer, and a gleaming black truck with chrome hub caps sat under the carport. A decal on the bumper said, "Reclaim your nation! Reclaim your heritage!"

Studying the roof, I could see that our list was accurate; no cable lines visible. A pit bull chained in the adjacent yard watched me with menace but was too hot to sound an alarm. I heard a television as I mounted the steps and rapped on the front door. A tall white man dressed in cargo shorts and a tank top opened the door. His head was shaved, and he looked to be in his mid-40s, with pronounced crow's feet around his dark eyes. Ill-defined prison tattoos lined his muscular arms, one of them a crude swastika.

The man glanced to his left at the neighbor's dog. "Good girl, Samantha. Definitely nothin' to worry about here." Then he swung his eyes to me. "What do you want?" he asked in a challenging tone.

"Good afternoon," I said, summoning my usual shtick. "From the outside of your home, it looks like you don't have cable TV yet. We're offering six months free and a huge reduction on any package you choose after that."

The man looked at me, his lips slowly curling into a smile. "I'm not interested in cable. There's not enough smut on it, which is what I prefer to watch."

He chuckled in a tone that I can only describe as sinister.

"That's not really true," I said. "There are a number of porn channels you can add to your basic package."

Our eyes met, and when he saw that I was not threatened by him, he smiled even more.

"Well, then come in and show me what you've got."

I stepped into the dim interior of the home. When my eyes adjusted, I could see that it was well-kept with new furnishings and a large color TV tuned to MTV. Annie Lennox of the Eurythmics sang, "Would I lie to you?" On a glass coffee table was a half empty bottle of Jose Cuervo. The air smelled faintly of booze and perspiration.

And that's when I saw her. She was standing in a hallway to my left, dressed in short cutoff jeans and a man's white dress shirt tied beneath her breasts to reveal her toned midriff. She was half his age, petite, her brunette hair tied back in a ponytail, and her face, free of makeup, was classically beautiful. Her hazel eyes met mine with a curious expression.

I guess I let my gaze linger too long, because the man chuckled in that menacing way.

"Meet my wife, Jewel," he said. "She's a cute little thing, isn't she?"

He walked over to stand by her, dwarfing her with his height, then made a show of grabbing her ass from behind. Beauty and the beast, for sure.

"Don't, Marco," she said, squirming.

He responded by pulling her closer and bending down to kiss her cheek. "Don't be embarrassed, baby. The man can recognize something prime when it's obvious."

Then he looked at me, his eyes boring into mine. "Before we talk about your cable package, how would you like to see a videotape of our wedding night? I think you'll love its graphic quality."

Jewel squirmed even more, trying unsuccessfully to free herself from his grasp.

By then, my skin was crawling. I started to back towards the door. "You know what, let me return first thing in the morning. I'll have more time then."

"What's the matter, man? I know you're interested. I saw it in your eyes."

I opened the front door and stepped onto the porch, glancing over my shoulder and muttering, "See you tomorrow."

I made my way quickly down the steps, Marco snickering behind me. I didn't stop until I reached my white Ford Mustang at the far end of the park. I slipped into the front seat and sat for a good five minutes, looking through the windshield, half expecting that skinhead to follow me, but the road was clear. I started the engine to let the AC take the edge off the heat.

I had encountered some strange situations in my door-to-door visits, but this was the oddest. Was Marco her pimp? Were they really married? I kept seeing her eyes as they had locked onto mine, and I felt compassion for her. How had she ended up in his Nazi grip?

Anyway, not my business, so I started the car and drove at a slow speed towards the exit, not letting my nerves push my foot too hard to the pedal. When I passed their home, I glanced over, but the door was closed and the curtains drawn. I let out my breath and drove another block.

Suddenly, in my peripheral vision, I saw someone running from between two mobile homes and approaching my passenger side. It was Jewel. She banged on the glass with her fist as I rolled down the window.

"Let me in," she gasped. "Please! I can't stay there another minute!"

If I had thought it through, who knows what I would have done. But instinct took over.

"Get in!"

She opened the door and swung into the seat, slamming it behind her. I stepped on the gas and headed for the exit, but it was too late. In my rearview mirror, I saw the black truck pull out of its driveway and head towards us.

"He'll kill me," she said. "And maybe you. We have to make it to the freeway! Turn right into that alley after the exit, then another right, and the onramp is close."

I followed her directions, sweating despite the AC.

"Fuck, fuck, fuck," I kept muttering.

I quickly followed her directions, but the black truck was gaining on us, so I goosed the Mustang, tires squealing as I saw the freeway entrance up ahead. I sped past a few cars, knifing my way between them as they honked their horns in protest. Then I raced up the ramp and merged into rush hour traffic.

"Shit, shit, shit," I muttered.

"Yep, a whole lot of shit," Jewel said. "Just keep going."

I looked into the rearview mirror but could no longer see the truck. I took Interstate 10, keeping my speed just under the limit, and didn't stop driving until I reached the Pacific Ocean.

Pasadena, California, December 24, 1996

The Christmas tree glittered with lights and tinsel as I took a sip of wine. Jules unwrapped one of his gifts, lifting a Buzz Lightyear action figure above his head.

"Aha!" he said. "To infinity and beyond!"

His twin sister, Jayden, laughed and lifted her own present, an action figure of Xena the Warrior Princess.

"And I will join you!" she said.

I smiled contentedly, grateful for how far our family had come in such a short time. The cable company had grown and met its goal of acquisition, distributing a healthy profit share to all our family members. And none of it would have been possible without my wife. She retrofitted herself with the right education, then took on the lion's share of the company's bookkeeping, taxes, and investments. She was the one who had successfully navigated us to this place and time.

She nuzzled up next to me on the couch where we were seated.

"We made some beautiful children."

"True," I said, "and I think they get both their looks and their smarts from their mother."

She chuckled and squeezed tighter against me.

"Once they get to bed," she said, "let's grab another glass of wine, go upstairs, and watch the video of our wedding night."

I pressed my lips against her ear.

"Sounds perfect, my Jewel. Just perfect."

High Country Hozho

Flagstaff, Arizona

In beauty, it is restored in beauty. – a Navajo proverb

Through the diner's window, I could see Humphrey's Peak in the distance. Rising to 12,633 feet, it's the crown of the San Francisco Volcanic Field, some of North America's most ancient geology. Andrew A. Humphreys was a Civil War General, so I prefer the Hopi title for the mountain, *Aaloosaktukwi*, meaning "its summit never melts."

It was now August and the snowpack was thin, clearing passage to the top on a popular trail. I planned to hike there the next morning.

I sipped my coffee and waited for the breakfast burrito recommended on Yelp. The place was popular, with most of the tables filled, a clatter of dishes and conversation.

The smell of bacon and biscuits filled the air.

Two months earlier, my wife, Liz, had seen my restlessness and sour mood. She'd endured my complaints about politics, the economy, and the inept administration at the high school where I taught. FUBAR, I muttered too often. I was out of whack, even more so than usual, and a deeper level of angst was seeping into my dreams at night. Finally, my grumbling was too much for Liz.

"Why don't you use your summer break to get out of here," she said. "You've always wanted to hit the road like the Jacks. What better time to do it?"

By Jacks she meant Kerouac and Reacher, two wanderers—one real, one fictional—that had always intrigued me. Liz knew that I lived vicariously through too many literary characters, reluctant to act on my own desires. She was laying down a gauntlet.

"You wouldn't mind holding down the fort?" I asked. We're childless, so that meant caring for our dog and cat.

She smiled and winked. "Mind? I'd be relieved to get rid of your moping for a while."

We both laughed and I made my decision. With very little foreplanning, I took our old Nissan Sentra and left our home in Fresno, California. Driving isn't romantic like hitchhiking, or using trains and buses, but I still let the road guide me. No set route, traveling at whim. I'd been to over a dozen states and seen some remarkable things. Now I was heading home.

But I still felt restless and out of balance, not what I expected after my mobile version of a walkabout. I feared this would be my default mood, and the thought of returning to work gave me claustrophobia. Liz deserved more. My students deserved more.

The server, a young Latina with multiple piercings and a bright smile, brought my breakfast and refilled my coffee. My eyes kept returning to the peak, imagining the next day's trek, when I had that sense that someone was watching me. I turned towards the dining counter, its swivel chairs lined with customers. There was a tall man wearing jeans, boots, and a Carhartt shirt, his long black hair in a ponytail. He looked to be in his mid-20s, certainly Native American, with high cheekbones and large, slightly almond-shaped eyes. He smiled at me as he slipped off his stool and made his way to my table, coffee cup in hand.

"I hope I'm not being rude," he said, "but I notice how you keep looking to the mountains."

Conversations with strangers had been some high points of my travels. "You're not being rude at all. I'm just thinking about my hike up Humphreys tomorrow morning. I'm looking forward to it."

He nodded. "It's a great climb. I was up there a couple weeks ago, something I wanted to do before going home. Now I've been to the top of all four sacred mountains."

"Four?"

"Yes. Mount Blanca to the east. Mount Taylor to the south. Mount Hesperus to the north, and these San Francisco Peaks to the west."

He gestured first through the window, then to the empty seat across from me. "Mind if I join you?"

"Not at all. I'd love the company."

He settled in and placed his cup on the table.

"My name's Thomas," he said, reaching his hand across the table to shake mine.

"Phil," I responded, returning his strong grip. "You mentioned going home. Where's that?"

"Shiprock. My family has roots that date back centuries."

"So, obviously you're Navajo."

"Navajo alone," he said with a wry smile.

"What does that mean?"

"That both sides of my family have never intermarried with other tribes or races. At least that's what we claim. It's a huge point of pride, especially for my mother's clan. Navajo snobs." He laughed. "How about you? Where are you from?"

"Fresno, California. I've been wandering around the country for a couple months, but I'm heading back. I'm a teacher, so I had a summer break. I'd always imagined taking an unstructured trip."

He nodded and sipped his coffee. "I'm thinking about teaching, but in a different way. I just graduated from Northern Arizona University with a degree in anthropology. I'd like to be a cultural interpreter, hopefully with the National Park Service."

"Sounds like a great goal."

He studied me for a few seconds. "I'm curious. Was all your wandering what you imagined it would be?"

His question felt like a tipping point. How much would I share with a stranger? I decided to let it all out.

"There's an old saying, 'wherever you go, there

you are.' I started this trek because I felt unbalanced. I had let so much of the conflict in our country get inside me. I felt powerless and insignificant, despite my wife's love. I know it sounds self-centered, but it was even hard to sleep at night. I thought that getting away for this time would help clear my head."

"But it didn't?"

"Not really. And now that I'm headed home, I have this depressing feeling that I'll just pick up where I left off."

He didn't say anything. We sat in silence as he turned his eyes to the distant peak. I began to wonder if I'd been too intimate, but I just waited. The breakfast crowd was thinning, with people leaving and cars pulling out of the parking lot.

Finally, he turned his eyes back to me. "Do you know the Navajo word *hozho*?"

"Vaguely."

"It's hard to translate, especially for Western minds. The closest *bilagáana* words would be balance or harmony. Our right relationship with nature, our community, and our inner selves. You could say it's the quality that Navajos hold most sacred."

I shook my head ruefully. "Harmony is rare in our world. I don't see it anywhere, and it doesn't help that I doom scroll too much on the web."

He chuckled. "I hear you. I can get wrapped up in it also, especially when I return home. There are so many challenges on the reservation and our people have such a painful history in relationship to this country. I have a sister who works as a nurse in one of our medical clinics. She keeps urging me to stay on the res and work to better our conditions, but I don't think it's my path. To be honest, I'm searching for a clearer direction."

I appreciated his candor. "I always encourage my students to find their own calling. The pressure to adopt scripts from our family and society is damn strong."

He nodded. "That's another reason I'm going home. To meet with my grandfather. He's an old sheep farmer but also one of the most respected medicine men on the res. Growing up, whenever he could see I was troubled, he insisted on helping me return to the old ways. Sometimes a sweat, sometimes a sing ceremony, sometimes just a reminder to say my daily prayers."

"Did it work?"

"Usually," he said with that wry smile again.

He reached into his pocket and pulled out what looked like a business card. "Anyway, I need to get on the road. Can I leave this with you?"

He handed it to me. "You probably know this famous prayer, the Blessing Way, but I find it helpful when I'm feeling restless or disturbed. I designed these to share with others I meet. A small piece of my culture."

The printing on the card was embossed, set against an image of a sunrise. It read, *With beauty before me I walk, with beauty behind me I walk, with beauty beneath me I walk, with beauty above me I walk, with beauty all around me I walk.*

I'd heard the words before, but not for a long time. "Thank you. I'll remember these few moments we shared."

He stood and reached to shake my hand. "So will

I. I'll be thinking about you on the trail tomorrow. You'll probably be near the summit as I pull into Shiprock."

Then he nodded and left. Through the window, I saw him get into an older Dodge pickup and merge onto the highway. I smiled and turned my gaze once again to the mountains.

I left the trailhead at dawn under a clear blue sky, determined to reach the top and return before the weather changed. Afternoon thunderstorms were always a threat, and I didn't want to be exposed on the peak.

The trail took me through shimmering aspen groves and meadows laced with lupine and columbine. Butterflies drifted among the flowers like blossoms with wings. The air was redolent with the smell of the soil, the grasses, and the trees, an intoxicating mix. At one switchback, just a few feet from the trail, a partridge eyed me with curiosity.

Mid-morning, I broke from the timber line and climbed the craggy volcanic stones of the final ascent, like mounting the stairs of an ancient temple jumbled by earthquakes. To my right, snow still clung to the slope. Swifts arrowed overhead, trapping alpine insects with precision.

The view from the summit was breathtaking. On the northwestern horizon was the rim of the Grand Canyon, carved over eons of time. To the northeast were the mesas of the Hopis who historically believed this peak is where kachinas live, the blessed bringers of rain.

The wind was brisk, buffeting my face. I'm not sure

how long I stood there drinking in the vistas, but slowly, thoughts of returning to the workaday schedule of my life began to crowd my mind, like traffic noise or conversation from a distant room that suddenly got louder. I pushed it away, thinking of my brief encounter with Thomas and the prayer he'd left with me.

I took a deep breath and surveyed the splendid view ahead of me. I turned my head to an equally magnificent panorama behind me. I looked beneath me at the multicolored volcanic stones, remnants of primordial eruptions. Then I lifted my eyes to the blue dome of the sky.

Beauty. All around me. Embracing me and moving through me, dissolving resistance to its presence. Time never really stands still, but it surely felt like it as I stood there for moments, for eternity, with only the wind in my ears and the sound of my own breathing.

When I finally began my descent, it was a pivot beyond words, a personal kenshō, and as I fell into my hiking cadence, I thought of some words from a review of Kerouac's *Dharma Bums*: "In the end, you won't remember the time you spent working in the office or mowing your lawn. Climb that goddamn mountain."

I started laughing so hard that some other hikers approaching me on the trail were startled.

"Having a good time?" one of them asked with a bemused smile.

"The time of my life," I responded.

The Final Incarnation

Mellow, easygoing, that's how Jamie's friends and family described him. Some tied it to his frequent pot smoking. Others linked it to his natural temperament, a Type Nine Enneagram, the Peacemaker, always seeking balance. His mother wished that her son had more ambition, but mostly she was relieved by the course of his life. She had worried constantly during his childhood. The schools he attended weren't as racially charged as those she had endured, but there were still clear divides. Jamie's mixed heritage, coupled with his quiet demeanor and ungainly height, were a magnet for bullying that his intelligence and kindness never quite overcame.

On the surface, Jamie seemed unscarred by his past, content with his job as host at a high-end restaurant. Both the staff and the patrons enjoyed his upbeat personality. On his days off, he indulged in his favorite hobbies: partaking of edibles or blunts, listening to his eclectic vinyl collection, and reading philosophers from across the centuries.

His girlfriend, Tasha, had a keen mind and sharp wit, but she was equally laid-back. An ideal date night was to get high, settle on the couch, stream a movie or cue up some tunes, then have leisurely sex afterwards. They had once listened to all four sides of Yes's *Tales from Topographic Oceans* without falling asleep, riding the musical sine waves together. They still laughed about that night. Jamie enjoyed the parameters of his relationship with Tasha. No pressures. No expectations. Perfect.

Not surprisingly, Jamie had turned a four-year degree at the local university into a sojourn with no end in sight. He was now in his early 30s, and if someone asked him when he planned to graduate, he would smile and say, "I'll get there. I'm just enjoying the trip."

On this particular morning, he was seated in a class called *The Existentialists*. They had covered Sartre, Kierkegaard, and were now reading Camus, starting with the Nobel Prize winner's seminal essay, *The Myth of Sisyphus*. As usual, Jamie found the conversation engaging. It ranged from abstract discussions of the absurdity of human existence to personal examples from people who felt they were pushing infernal stones up hills in their personal lives. Both the original Greek myth and Camus's interpretation came alive.

Existentialist tenets resonated with Jamie. Despite the unflappable mask he wore around others, even Tasha, anxiety about the direction of his life sometimes gripped him. He knew that his long educational journey was a quest to discover some meaning that eluded him. This was his stone, the one he rolled upwards over and over, never getting a satisfying sense of who he was or what he was called to do. When those feelings of unfulfillment became overwhelming, he took refuge in THC. It was a medicine that dampened the dread, but it left him wondering what was on the other side of his soul's dark night.

One guy in the existentialist class named Ian always had something unusual to say. Jamie had met him in other courses and recognized a fellow traveler on the long track of schooling. He felt a kinship with him.

"To me, one of the symbols of this Sisyphean task," said Ian, "is humankind's constant struggles for justice throughout the centuries. Consider how many times people have rebelled against oppressive economic and political systems in one historical age after another."

"Countless times," said a woman named Romana. "But when I think of those struggles, Camus's notion of absurdity is spot-on. How much have we really gained as a species? We're still warring. The poor still get crumbs from the 2%. Politicians still traffic in their own power with little regard for average citizens. It seems pointless and absurd."

Jamie felt compelled to speak. "Existentialism isn't nihilism, Romana. That's why I agree with Sartre's concept of the existentialist hero. Our ability to act for the common good brings meaning to this life. We can become protagonists in the best sense of the word. Sartre called existentialism a new form of humanism."

"I agree with Jamie," said Ian. "If you look at recent social movements like Occupy Wall Street, Black Lives Matter, or No Kings, I think we've made real gains. I think we're elevating our collective consciousness."

Romana snorted. "Our collective consciousness? Elevated? In our country, what about the backlash from white privilege, wrapping itself in the American and Christian flags? It's the same sick dance over and over. It's a boulder of absurdity. And I don't even think it gets far up the hill before it slams back down on our heads."

Ian was nodding. "I hear you. But it's too easy to be cynical, and cynicism is cancerous. If you knew the heroic struggles I've seen while leading people through past lives under hypnosis, you might feel differently."

"Remember our class covenants," interjected Professor Sanchez, a transplant from Mexico with fierce intelligence and a strong will. "We agreed to stay out of the realms of religion and speculative fantasy."

"I know, I know," said Ian, "but with all those incarnations I've witnessed. . ."

"Ian..." cautioned the instructor.

Ian laughed, threw up his hands in surrender, and the conversation moved to other things. But Ian's comment lingered in Jamie's mind. As they were going out the door after class, he tapped Ian on the shoulder.

"What did you mean by working with past lives through hypnosis?"

"Call it my lifetime's obsession," said Ian. "After I got my formal training in hypnosis, I took a seminar on past-life regression. It fascinated me how people who had never even considered the idea ended up discovering these incredible experiences buried in their unconscious memories. All it took was a willingness to peel back the layers."

"Do you still experiment?"

Ian raised his eyebrows and smiled in a bemused way. "Absolutely. Are you interested?"

Looking back later, Jamie wasn't sure why he was so intrigued, but in a way that was completely out of character, he blurted, "I am."

"Cool," said Ian. "Give me a call and we'll set up a time."

They exchanged numbers and Jamie promised to make contact.

The First Incarnation

As Jamie drove towards the address Ian had given him, he replayed the previous night's discussion with Tasha.

"I don't get it," she said. "I understand being curious about past lives, or even hypnosis, but why would you submit yourself to some guy you barely know? Have you read about this practice? It's been discredited by legit therapists who use hypnosis to really help people."

"I read that, but I don't think it's dangerous. Besides, what if this opens some realizations about my life that I've needed to connect with for too long?"

Tasha shook her head, pulling back her dark hair. She downplayed her beauty, but when she got emotional, her eyes flashed with alluring vitality.

"Is this the new Jamie? Off on psychic adventures without chemical assistance? It's not like you to leave your comfort zone."

She laughed in a forced way and shook her head

again. "Anyway, I don't see why you would give some random guy access to your mind. What if he doesn't play nicely in there?"

Jamie swallowed. He did have some trepidation, but he had grown tired of playing it safe. A nagging part of his brain told him he was pissing away his life with nothing to show for it. This seemed like an adventure, maybe even that key to greater meaning that was always out of reach. He was determined to carry it out.

He turned into the driveway of Ian's modest bungalow. It was well-kept, painted an off-yellow, the lawn neatly trimmed. A gurgling fountain and flower beds bursting with spring color adorned the yard. As he stepped out of his car, he could smell the blossoms and hear bees buzzing at their pollinator chores.

He walked up to the door and pressed the intercom button. A voice crackled over the speaker.

"Welcome, Jamie. Just a second."

Jamie heard footsteps approaching from within, then Ian opened the door with a smile

"Come on in. I'd appreciate you taking off your shoes."

Jamie slipped them off, then followed Ian into the main living room. Like the exterior, it was clean, nearly gleaming. Along the walls were enlarged photographs of sacred sites from around the world: the Sikhs' Golden Temple in the Punjab, Angkor Wat, Machu Picchu, and Teotihuacán.

"Beautiful photos," said Jamie. "Did you take them?"

Ian nodded. "I love to travel and chronicle my journeys. Another avocation of mine. Several of these remind me of transcendent moments. Not just because of their beauty, but because I felt a sort of communion, a connection to those who occupied those holy places." He laughed. "Does that sound odd?"

"Not at all," said Jamie. "Honestly, I envy you a bit. The only trips I've taken have been through the portal of a television or at the end of a joint."

Ian laughed again. "I'm glad you're here. Are you anxious?"

"A bit, but I'm ready to experiment."

"Okay, then let me give you a few disclaimers."

"I'm listening."

"First of all, I'm sure you're aware that most people discredit this practice. They're the same ones who discredit *any* avenue of psychic exploration outside the norms of what we can prove. Also, you need to know that I'm not one who religiously holds to reincarnation. I don't press my beliefs on anyone."

"Then what got you so interested in this?"

"It's pretty simple. During my training in hypnosis, I allowed someone to lead me back to what I consider my own former lives. I can tell you about it another time if you'd like, but not today."

"I'd love to hear that. Is there anything else I need to know?"

"Just a bit about my method. It's a blend of hypnotherapy and guided imagery. You'll be in a mild hypnotic state, able to follow my suggestions, but you'll also be able to speak with me about them. Is that okay with you?"

"It is. I'm ready."

"All right then. Follow me."

He led Jamie down a short hallway, then through a door on the right. The space had clearly been two former bedrooms, the partition demolished to create a studio. The walls displayed more gorgeous photos—the Pyramid of Giza, Stonehenge, the Alhambra, and the Parthenon. At the center of the room was a massage table, deeply cushioned with a pillow at one end. Faint ambient music played from speakers positioned in the corners. The air smelled of sandalwood incense.

"Is that music by Steve Roach?" asked Jamie

"Yep," said Ian with obvious surprise. "No one has ever recognized it. It's from *Dreamtime Return*, Roach's immersion in Australia's aboriginal culture. You a fan of his?"

"I'm a fan of many genres. My musical tastes might give you whiplash they're so diverse. Soundtracks for those journeys I take from my living room couch."

Ian chuckled. "Nice. I love how Roach explores the aboriginal concept of time."

"What do you mean?"

"Our Western minds think of time in such a linear way. Today is today, yesterday was yesterday, tomorrow will be tomorrow. But Indigenous Australians conceive of time as circular. The past, the present, and the future are interconnected, and those who have gone before us are always present. I have found this to be true in both my experiments and my personal life. Time is flexible. Fluid."

Jamie nodded. "Interesting. I've always thought of time as a dimension we poorly understand. Maybe Einstein was right when he said time is an illusion."

"Not an illusion, just bendable," said Ian, looking away for an instant, then back at Jamie.

Jamie was still scanning the photos in the room. A few were different than the others, like blown-up newspaper clippings, a bit yellowed, the kind you might find in a museum exhibit. One caught his attention. It showed a group of people standing on top of the Berlin Wall, the Brandenburg Gate behind them. Jamie had seen similar images in a history class, and he knew that the event took place in the late 1980s. Yet right there, in the middle of the protesters raising their fists and tearing down the wall, was Ian. He looked the same as he did this very moment.

"That's you on top of the Berlin Wall, isn't it?"

Ian was slow to respond, his eyes averted from Jamie's. "Yes. That's me. A thrilling moment for all of us."

"How come you don't look any older than today? Did someone Photoshop the image?"

Ian finally looked back at Jamie with a remote expression. "I guess I just have good genes. Anyway, let's get started. Go ahead and lie down on the table. Get yourself comfortable."

Feeling even more unsettled, but determined to see this through, Jamie climbed onto the platform, nestled into the cushions, and eased his head back against the pillow. His long legs stuck out from the end just a bit.

Ian was silent for a full moment.

"Now," he finally said, "just close your eyes and follow my voice."

Jamie did so and waited. The background music ceased, and Ian said nothing for another moment as Jamie heard only the ebb and flow of his own breathing.

"I want you to imagine that you are floating above the rooftop of your childhood home," said Ian in a gentle voice. "Take your time and visualize as much detail as possible."

Jamie concentrated on the suburban house his family had lived in most of his life. He saw the flat roof covered with white rocks. He saw the expansive redwood decking at the rear of the property and the blue water of the swimming pool it surrounded. He saw the many trees his father, an insurance executive, had lovingly planted—liquid amber, eucalyptus, elm, and sycamore. He saw the clubhouse his father had built for him and his brothers in a side yard.

"Keep visualizing," coaxed Ian. "Let every detail grow sharper."

Jamie focused further. Now he could see the many Talavera pots his mother had planted with succulents. The bright colors of the pottery as well as the exotic blooms of the cacti crystallized in his mind's eye. He saw the Adirondack chairs on the decking with their red and yellow pillows, and the hummingbird feeders hanging from the trees.

"Now," said Ian, "imagine that you are floating even higher. Feel yourself becoming weightless and ascending as the scene below grows smaller."

Jamie saw the house receding, its colors growing dimmer.

"And let yourself go…"

Jamie suddenly felt suspended in what seemed like a gray vapor or cloud that surrounded him. Slowly the mist began to recede and the first sensation he had, with a clarity that startled him, was sunlight beating hot and heavy on his back.

"Tell me what you feel," said Ian.

"Sunlight scorching my shoulders."

"Scan your body. What are you wearing?"

Jamie examined himself.

"My skin is black and I'm barebacked. My pants are old and faded. My shoes seem to be made of canvas, and they're so frayed that one of my toes is sticking out. I'm holding a short-handled hoe in my hands."

"Good. Any more details? Look around you."

Jamie lifted his eyes and realized he was in the furrow of a field. He could smell the fecund soil, and it startled him. He had not expected his senses to be so acute.

"I'm working in a field."

"Are there others?"

Jamie surveyed the scene and saw other laborers, most of them Black but also a few Whites. A cacophony of sounds assailed him: people grunting, a clanking of tools hitting stones, crows squawking from the trees that bordered the field, and then, in the distance, a cracking sound. He looked farther down the furrow and saw a White man sitting atop a horse, holding a whip in one hand, a shotgun holstered on his horse's flank.

"I'm enslaved. There are others here, both men and women, and there's a man on horseback keeping everyone in line."

"What emotions are you having?"

Emotions? thought Jamie, never considering that he would be so conscious in a scene like this. But the answer was immediate and strong, like bile rising from his stomach.

"I have this burning rage inside me. It seems like a feeling that's been smoldering in my bones forever. It's almost overwhelming."

Just as he said that, he saw a man leap up from one of the furrows and begin running toward the tree line. The guard on the horse didn't hesitate. He lifted his shotgun, took aim, and fired. The fleeing slave's body contorted with the impact, like an unstrung marionette, and he fell bloodied into the dirt.

"No!" shouted Jamie, jerking himself upwards and out of hypnosis.

———

"That's a fucking trip," said Tasha. "You could actually see, smell, and hear all those things?"

"As if they were right here and now."

"Jeez. What did Ian say when you woke up after the gunshot?"

"He didn't seem surprised, as if visions like that are normal. He just asked me to describe it again, writing down my responses on his laptop. Then he said it was up to me if I wanted to come back for a second session."

"It's too weird to wrap my head around," said Tasha. "I'm not closed-minded. You know that. But you? A slave in a former life?"

She laughed in a strained way.

"What's so funny?" he asked, feeling a flash of anger.

Tasha saw it in his eyes. "I'm not laughing at you, just the strangeness of it. Most people who have experienced injustice in their lives seem motivated to fight for change. They seem driven or fanatical. You're one of the most levelheaded people I've ever met. It's one of the reasons I love you. I'm so tired of all the fighting in our society. Right and left, Republican and Democrat, class against class, race against race, religion against religion. Has any of it helped our progress?"

"I hear you. But what if I've been so laid-back that I've lost a connection to my passion? What if I'm like a sleepwalker? What if I don't really know who I am or where I've come from? My family never gave me any sense of my roots."

Tasha shook her head. "Who is this person talking to me? I'm not sure you should go back."

"I have to," snapped Jamie. "I *have* to go back."

The Second Incarnation

"Tell me what you see," said Ian.

"I'm standing on the boardwalk of a town. The architecture around me is colonial style, and there's a church steeple in the distance. I think I'm in New England. The roads are dirt and horses and buggies are passing by. All kinds of stores line the street. A mercantile, an oil outlet, a bakery, a tavern. I can hear the snorts of horses, people talking and laughing, some kind of piano music from an open door to my right."

"What else? What do you look like and what are you wearing?"

Jamie studied himself. "My skin is white. I'm wearing a work apron of some kind. It's covered in black spots, and my hands have smudges of the same color. I think it must be ink."

"Look behind you. What do you see?"

"I'm standing in front of a printing shop. Through the window I can see long tables covered with small blocks and stacks of paper. There are cabinets lining the walls, and some kind of large machine, probably the press, in the rear. Two men and a woman are assembling things at the tables."

"Keep letting the details materialize."

Jamie focused on some letters etched into the glass of the entrance door. "The door says, 'Oldfield Print Shop, James Oldfield, Proprietor, For all your printing needs.'"

"James Oldfield. Is that your name?"

"Yes, it is," said Jamie with sudden certainty. "I own this shop."

He then noticed something posted on the front window.

"There's a paper glued to the window. A flyer or handbill of some kind. It says, 'Union with Freemen, Not Union with Slaveholders! Three million of your fellow beings are in chains and the Church and Government sustain this horrible system of oppression. Join us for an Anti-Slavery Meeting on April 17, 7:00 p.m. at First Unitarian Church. Special address by James Oldfield, candidate for city mayor. Come and learn your duty to yourselves, the slaves, and God!'"

"So, a printer, a mayoral candidate, and an abolitionist."

Jamie felt his pulse beginning to rise. "Yes!"

He turned at a noise from behind him. A fashionably dressed man and woman were approaching along the boardwalk, the man in a three-piece suit and bowler hat, the woman in a voluminous brocade dress with a floral design. They didn't look at Jamie until they were almost upon him, and at that moment the man leaned in close to Jamie and whispered, "agitator dog," then quickly walked away.

Jamie watched the man's back as he retreated—a gesture of indifference, even arrogance—and he felt his fists clench with the same rage he had experienced in the first incarnation. He stepped toward the man, intent on knocking him to the ground and pummeling his face until it was bloodied...

"What's happening!" exclaimed Ian, the sharpness of his tone awakening Jamie.

———————

"Unbelievable," said Tasha, shaking her head with concern. "That was more vivid than the first time. It sounds like you wanted to kill that guy on the boardwalk. What have you gotten yourself into? What did Ian say?"

"It was sort of odd this time. He just nodded with this knowing smile, like he was amused by the whole thing, or that it confirmed some theory of his."

"This is getting stranger and stranger. Have you done a background check on this guy?"

"Of course. I couldn't find him listed anywhere as a hypnotist, but he's all over social media. A lot of pictures of him with activists in Occupy Wall Street and Black Lives Matter. He even has some links to articles about Antifa. You can see him clearly at various protests, including the one following George Floyd's death. But that's not surprising. When I've heard him speak in my classes, you could tell he was super liberal."

"What else?"

"Just a lot of other photos from his travels around the world. I saw a fair amount of them on the walls of his home. The only surprising thing on Facebook and Instagram was that some of those photos showed him involved in protests in Germany, Argentina, and Brazil."

"He sounds like a true believer," said Tasha. "Has he ever tried to enlist you in his causes?"

"Never. Not a word."

"How old is he?"

"It's hard to tell. Could be in his late thirties, maybe early forties. He's youthful but he also seems older than he looks. And…"

Jamie caught himself in mid-sentence.

"What?" asked Tasha.

Jamie sighed. "I haven't told you one of the strangest things. There are photos on his wall that seem to be from actual historical events. The first time I was there, I noticed one from the tearing down of the Berlin Wall. Yesterday I saw one from the Montgomery Bus Boycott, Martin Luther King, Jr. and his wife Loretta marching arm in arm with others."

"So he's a history buff. What's so strange about that?"

"What's strange is that those two events took place 35 years ago and 67 years ago. I did the math. And in each of them you can clearly see Ian right there in the scene."

"Were they altered? Did someone Photoshop him into them? Like those segments from *Forrest Gump* where he shows up at actual moments in history."

"I don't think so. They look too real. When I asked him about them, he was evasive, just saying that youthfulness is something he inherited."

Tasha shook her head vehemently. "Isn't that enough to make you stay away? I don't like this at all. What the hell is going on with this guy? My Spidey Sense is telling me you should cut him loose. Who knows what his ultimate motive is. For my sake, will you please stop going? You've had a couple of vivid trips. Isn't that enough?"

Jamie looked down at his lap, unable to counter the intensity in Tasha's eyes. "One more time. Then I'll stop."

"Please look at me," she said. "We have a comfortable life. We love each other in our own ways. I care about you more than you know. I never really ask you for anything. I never make demands. But right now, I am. Don't go back. I don't think this is safe."

Jamie met her eyes, and for one of the few times in their relationship, he felt defiant, shaking his head. "I'm not interested in comfort right now. What if my comfort is built on the backs of others? What if it *still* is? The same goes for you. I know your views on things. I know you pride yourself on not taking sides. I've always gone with that flow, but it's not working for me anymore. In only two sessions, I've seen things I'll *never* forget. Are these actually my former lives or just a hypnotic dream state? You know what? It really doesn't matter. They're real at some level that needs to change me and I welcome it!"

He stopped, realizing he was shouting. He brought it down a notch. "Anyway, it's not your choice. I'm going one more time whether you like it or not."

Tasha suddenly stood. "Then you'll have to debrief with someone else."

Her tone was sharper than he'd ever heard. She turned, grabbed her overnight backpack, and made her way out the front door.

Jamie was a bit stunned, but her departure only galvanized his resolve. Sitting on the couch in silence, images from the first two sessions played through his mind: the sun on his skin, the crack of the whip, the blast of the shotgun, the ink staining his clothes and hands, the poster on the window of his print shop, the infuriating remark from the man along the boardwalk. If this was the awakening of the purpose that had eluded him, he wanted to be fully aroused.

He usually smoked a joint before bed to help him sleep, but on this night he was sober as he lay on his back and stared at the ceiling fan. Emotions from the argument with Tasha roiled beneath the surface. He got up and went to the bathroom, staring at his face in the mirror. In a sudden burst of rage, he slammed his fist into the glass, splintering his reflection into a puzzle he wasn't sure he could reassemble.

The Final Incarnation

"This is going to be my final session," said Jamie. "I'm grateful to you. It's been *more* than interesting, but I have enough information to think about for the rest of this lifetime."

Ian looked closely at him, scanning his face as if searching for clues, then noticing the bandages on his knuckles.

"What happened to your hand?"

Jamie looked into Ian's eyes. "It's nothing. Let's do this."

Ian smiled as if Jamie had somehow shared a secret. "Okay, then let's get started. And thanks for helping me with my research."

Jamie nodded and eased back on the pillow. Ian took him once again into the sky above his childhood home, then the clouds, and this time as the fog dispersed, he found himself in the midst of what seemed like a riot, causing his body to tense. Explosions and shouting voices filled the air.

"What is it?" said Ian. "What do you see?"

Jamie scanned the scene, immediately thinking of Tasha's warnings as fear started to grip him.

"I'm with a crowd on an inner-city street. There are skyscrapers rising above us. The people around me are young and old, of all different races. They're carrying bottles, rocks, or clubs in their hands, and they're chanting something."

"Can you make out the words?"

"Yes. Down with the Imperium! Human beings will not be your slaves!"

"What about yourself? What do you look like?"

Jamie looked down. His skin was black, and he was dressed in an old pair of jeans and a T-shirt. The shirt had a symbol that looked like a combination rainbow and lightning bolt encircling three words in bright red: *Humans, not AI!* He was carrying a baseball bat in this right hand.

"I'm wearing…" Jamie began to say, but his words were cut short as the crowd swelled and pushed him along in its tide. He looked in the direction they were heading. Buildings burned in the distance. A phalanx of riot police dressed in full battle gear was marching towards them in locked unison. They moved with a jerky mechanical precision, not human, as if connected to the same power source. People began to chant even louder, *Down with the Imperium!*

Jamie had no choice but to be swept along with the crowd. He lifted his eyes and saw a message flashing on a digital billboard: "The Imperium requires your allegiance on this day, July 15, 2092."

Jamie blinked and shook his head. 2092? The future? Not the past? How was that possible? His fear turned into panic.

"Ian! Ian!"

No response. He tried to shake himself out of hypnosis, but it didn't work.

"Ian!" he shouted again, and a response came from nearby.

"I'm right here!" called a voice to his right, barely audible through the noise of the crowd.

Jamie looked along the front line of advancing

protesters and instantly spotted the hypnotist, who was dressed in the same logoed shirt. Ian smiled fiercely, nodding his head then gesturing forward with the bat in his hand.

"What the fuck?" shouted Jamie, but Ian's face was swallowed by the crowd, and all he could hear were the chanting voices and explosions in the distance. Smoke from the fires had descended on both sides of the advancing lines, stinging his eyes and coating his throat.

He gripped his bat harder. The riot police appeared through the haze like a legion of mechanized orcs, and suddenly his panic and fear were replaced by that primordial rage from his other incarnations. It rose out of his organs and bones until it erupted into a cry from deep in his lungs.

"Down with the Imperium!" he shouted.

Then he surged forward, brandishing his bat above his head.

The Grunt

January 2017

When the student is ready, the teacher will appear – a
Buddhist saying

On the day I met Nadia, Fort Jackson had a rare dusting of
snow, which only spurred the drill sergeants. *Nothing
like inclement weather to harden the grunts!* was their
motto. I could hear platoons shouting cadences outside my
office window. Rain or shine, the post trained 1,200 soldiers
each 10-week cycle. Some of them would find themselves
in the deserts of Afghanistan.

I was early in my career as a chaplain, rank of captain,
counseling a stream of privates from across America. Even
this early in the morning, the line of those seeking my
assistance wrapped around the building. They had recently
arrived amidst the harsh realities of boot camp, and some

of them were panicking. They would claim they needed a discharge for emotional, physical, or familial reasons. I would give them a safe place to vent, even cry, without the ridicule of peers or NCOs, but unless they presented a true hardship or exhibited mental illness, I would get them back on the trail, saying *you can do this, you're capable of more than you imagine*. I felt like I was on autopilot.

Nadia was last in line, and when she entered my office, I instantly sensed something different. She was squared-away, carrying no real or fabricated signs of fatigue. She wore her uniform well, her last name—Rivera—on the patch above her pocket. There was a crispness to her step, and her dark eyes, slightly Asian-looking, fixed on mine with burning intensity. She could have been 18 years old or 38. She had that kind of presence.

She saluted, though it wasn't required indoors. "Thanks for seeing me, sir. I'm sure there are many others that need more help than I do."

"Perhaps," I responded, "but why do you say that?"

"Because I'm not here to ask for a discharge or to complain about the sergeants. They're just doing their job."

"Then why *are* you here?"

She paused, looked away for an instant, then made eye contact again. "I guess you could say I have a theological question."

I chuckled, which raised her eyebrows.

"You find that funny, sir?"

"A bit. Most privates don't even know the meaning of the word theological. Have a seat."

She settled into the chair on the opposite side of my

desk. She looked briefly into her lap, then raised her head again. "Humorous or not, can I ask the question I came with?"

"Fire away."

Her eyes focused more intently. "Would you say that the Jesus you represent is perhaps the most nonviolent person in history? I mean, he didn't resist when they crucified him. He kept his disciples from fighting back. And just before he died, he asked his god to forgive the people who were torturing him."

It certainly wasn't what I expected, and my expression told her so. "That's true. It's why Old Testament prophecies said he would be known as the Prince of Peace."

She made a strange sound, like a deep, animalistic grunt.

"Excuse me? Did you say something?"

"No sir, it's just a noise I make to remind myself that the world is FUBAR."

The back of my neck prickled. "That's an extreme statement. Explain what you mean."

"With all due respect, sir, I've done a lot of reading in my life. I know that even Gandhi respected Jesus as a prophet of nonviolence. But you and other chaplains wear that silver cross on your uniform. You represent a country that is the mightiest military power on the planet. One that sells more weapons around the world than any other nation."

She made that strange, grunting sound again, her eyes locked on mine.

I felt a bit defensive, and it galled me that I let her get under my skin. *Who is this person?* I thought. *What's really going on*? *I have no reason to justify myself to a recruit.*

I calmed myself and assumed an air of authority, a posture I disliked in other officers. "I'm curious. With that level of judgment about America, why would you enlist?"

"Pretty simple, sir. I need help funding my education. No one else is going to do that for me."

"And you're willing to risk combat assignment?"

"I doubt that will happen with my job choice."

"Which is?"

"17S. Cyber Operations Specialist."

I nodded. I knew she had scored highly on her ASVAB test to qualify. I also knew her advanced training would take place at two locales—the Naval Air Station in Pensacola, then the Cyber School at Fort Gordon, Georgia. I looked again at her name tag, then at the slight almond-shape of her eyes and the darkness of her skin.

"Are you willing to share some more about your background?" I asked.

Despite her bulletproof exterior, she seemed eager for someone to listen. And so I did, prompting her with questions, intrigued by this unique woman.

She grew up in a housing project of East Baltimore, where drugs, gang activity, and violence were common. Her father was Puerto Rican, her mother of mixed Black and Filipino descent, both with low-paying jobs. They were decent parents that warned Nadia and her younger sister to avoid the negative influences of the street. Nadia took their advice to heart, but her sister got snared in gang life. That was when their mother, who had battled depression for years, withdrew even more from the family. One day, Nadia woke up to find her gone. When she asked her father what had happened, his face turned to stone. "She went back to the Philippines," he said.

Nadia paused in her story and made that grunting sound again, this time longer and more pronounced.

"That's a hard blow to be abandoned by your mother," I said. "Is that the hardship you wanted to share?"

"I didn't intend to share *any* of this when I came in here. But since you ask, my mom's disappearance definitely contributes to my main question. How do we have hope when the world around us is so fucked up?"

"That's a broad condemnation."

Her face took on an angry cast. "Not really, sir. At least from my perspective. Like I already said, Christians following a nonviolent Jesus but supporting a war machine. Hardworking citizens like my parents barely able to survive financially while rich politicians in Washington feed off the people and argue with each other like junior high students. A mother that abandons her children. A planet that is groaning from all our waste. More and more animals heading towards extinction. A climate growing warmer by the year. And no one in power seems to really give a damn. Who needs to watch a Netflix movie about some future dystopia? It's already here."

Whoa. Her vocabulary and intelligence amazed me, my neck prickling even harder. We looked at each other in silence. It was like she was trying to read my eyes and determine whether I was part of the problem or part of the solution. Or maybe if she could trust me.

"I've never heard a solider speak to me like this," I

said. "Where did you receive your education?"

Her expression shifted. "Now *that* is what you believers might call a miracle."

"How so?"

"I had this teacher in high school. Ms. Samuels. How she ever survived at that shithole of a campus is beyond me. She started this club called Sojourners. It was a group of us that would read literature and philosophy and have discussions. We also went on field trips to museums, film festivals, and lectures. Most of my peers thought I was a nerd."

"Sounds more like college."

"Exactly! Ms. Samuels was *so* inspiring, and she was hard on us. Sort of like a drill sergeant. Read, read, read, she kept saying. Think, think, think. Expand your minds, expand your life."

"Seems like her advice paid off in your case."

"In some ways, yeah. But no one tells you that the more you learn, the more messed up the world will appear."

She grunted once more, then suddenly stood up from her chair so swiftly it startled me.

"Sir, my apologies for keeping you so long. Thank you for listening."

"It's not a problem…" I began to say, but she had already saluted, turned on her heels, and left my office.

———————

That night, sipping a beer in my quarters, I replayed our conversation. It might have seemed treasonous to tell her how much I resonated with her. The deconstruction of my own worldview had begun years before, shortly after I joined the Army, a slow fissure working its way through one belief after another.

I recalled some of my final talks with Emily, the woman I thought I would marry. I was fresh out of seminary when we dated, and I was leaning towards the chaplaincy, encouraged by friends and relatives who thought it would suit me. Emily, however, was veering in a more liberal direction, working on a master's degree in political science.

"It's not that I think you wouldn't be good for the job," she said, "but can you really support what we're doing in Afghanistan? Or what we've done throughout the Middle East? We criticize other countries for intervening unilaterally in the affairs of other nations, then we do it ourselves with impunity."

I countered with my usual arguments about just war, the support of lesser evils in a fallen world, my chance to minister to soldiers who needed support no matter what uniform they wore, but Emily and I drifted further apart. Our breakup was inevitable.

I took another sip, remembering a recent candlelight vigil for a young soldier named Jason, killed in the Registan Desert outside Kandahar. He was 19. Since his family lived near Fort Jackson, a fellow chaplain from a more conservative denomination presided at the memorial. He wore his fundamentalist beliefs like a flak jacket, and I had always found him irritating. He spoke these words to those of us gathered on that cool fall evening.

"Tonight you must remember that two people died for you. One was Jesus Christ himself, our Lord and Savior, and the other was Jason!"

Even as others nodded in agreement, that phrase stung me like the *keisaku* stick used by Zen abbots to awaken drowsy monks. What a blasphemous paradox, I thought, a twisted co-opting of faith that extended all the way back to Constantine. Jesus as a supporter of an American war in a faraway desert, where a young man senselessly died in his prime. Not the Jesus who championed nonviolence from the first moments of his ministry to his last breath on the cross, saying, "Father forgive them, for they don't know what they are doing." Not the Jesus who said "love your enemy" at the cost of his own life.

Like Nadia, I had read my share of Gandhi, and at that moment I remembered the gist of something he said—how it was a tragedy that people who followed Jesus, the Prince of Peace, practiced so little of his nonviolent beliefs in their lives.

Every day the bucket draws through the well. One day the bottom drops out.

———————

I kept track of Nadia in the following weeks, visiting sites where her platoon was training. I saw her rappelling down towers, low crawling in the mud under barbed wire, marching in cadence during drills. She noticed me on one occasion, and I saw a smile on her face.

Then, one afternoon, a staff sergeant told me that the commander had approved Nadia for a three-day hardship leave. Her sister had died in a drive-by shooting near their home in Baltimore, and Nadia had requested to see me before she left.

This time, when she entered, her bravado was gone. There was a harried look to her face as she sat silently.

"I'm so sorry for your loss, Private Rivera."

She grunted once, twice, and a third time as tears rolled down her cheeks.

"Just call me Nadia, sir."

I nodded. There was nothing I could say, and long ago I had learned that being present is sometimes the best we can do. We sat in silence for quite a while, late afternoon sunlight slanting through my office window. Two wayfarers at a bus stop in eternity, just sharing the space of being human. She would look down occasionally into her lap, then back up at me, and the haunted depth in her eyes is something I will never forget.

———————

The following week, the First Sergeant of Nadia's company pulled me aside.

"Sir?

"Yes, sergeant."

"That recruit you helped, Nadia Rivera, came back from her leave and it's a bit strange."

"Strange? What do you mean?"

"She's wired, sir. She's performing above and beyond on every level. Helping other privates, taking on extra duties. It's like she's manic or high on adrenaline 24/7."

"People deal with grief in different ways."

"That's true," said the sergeant, 'but I haven't seen a

reaction like this since my time in the desert. It's like a form of PTSD. I hope she doesn't burn out."

A few days before graduation, I got a call from the battalion commander.

"Chaplain, that private Rivera you've counseled is in the hospital. She's suffering from dehydration and a sprained lower back. She passed out during one of our drill exercises on the parade grounds. It seems to me and others that something more serious is going on, something with her nerves. I need you to visit her and give me your assessment. Is she fit to move on to advanced training, or should we muster her back to civilian life? We don't want to kick this can down the road for someone else to deal with. Am I clear?"

"Yes, sir, I'll let you know what I think."

When I entered the hospital room, Nadia was hooked up to IV lines and a vitals monitor. Her eyes turned to greet me. Gone was the haunted look I had seen after her sister's death, replaced by something that resembled defiance.

"Let me guess, sir. They want you to see if I'm still fit for duty."

I nodded. "Are you?"

She glanced toward the ceiling, then shifted her eyes to me.

"If you mean, will I work hard at my assignments, yes. If you mean, can I still take care of myself, yes. If you mean, will I be the best Cyber Operations Specialist I can be, yes. But if you mean, am I a misfit in this fucked up world that no one seems able to make sense of, well…"

Her eyes strayed again to the ceiling. Her speech was indeed rushed, despite the fatigue she must have been feeling, but I had decided before I came to her bedside that her future would be in *her* hands, not mine or the impersonal green machine of Army bureaucracy. I felt she had earned that right given the trials she had already endured.

"Well, Private Rivera, in my mind you're good to go. The Army is privileged to have someone with your intelligence, strength, and experience."

She tried not to show it, but a few tears leaked from the corners of her eyes. She quickly wiped them away and gave me an appraising glance.

"I guess this is the point where you chaplains offer to say a prayer."

I smiled. And then I grunted. Once, twice, three times.

Her eyes opened wider and she grunted in return.

She grinned, I grinned, and then we both started laughing. It must have sounded a bit hysterical because a nurse stuck his head in the door.

"Is everything alright here, sir?"

I turned to him. "That is *the* question, sergeant. I guess we'll have to wait and see."

He looked at me quizzically and Nadia and I both laughed again.

The Beauty Seer

Her day would climax with an unimagined nightmare, but Alma Fuentes was lighthearted as she unlocked her storefront entrance at 9:00 a.m., a ritual as regular as sunrise.

She stepped outside to make sure her hanging sign wasn't tilted, dusting it with a red bandanna. Orange and black letters announced, "The Beauty Seer, by Appointment or Walk-ins Welcome," her phone number beneath.

She glanced along the sidewalk towards downtown San Antonio, early sunlight slanting through gaps in the buildings. It would be a typical summer day in South Texas, tourists along the Riverwalk braving extreme heat and humidity. Grackles whistled from nearby trees, and the exhaust from a recent bus lingered in the air.

Further along the street, Alma could see Carlos, a homeless man on his panhandling circuit, holding court with the voices in his head. Sometimes he would stand on the sidewalk across from her shop and protest her practice, holding a sign that read "Repent from witchcraft! Only Jesus can save you!" She talked to him once, trying to explain that her craft had nothing to do with the dark arts, but he refused to listen. He fixated on the word seer, quoting an obscure verse from the Old Testament prophet Micah: "The seers shall be disgraced, and the diviners put to shame; they shall all cover their lips." Impressed by his knowledge of scripture, she tried to show him that seers were used positively by other Biblical characters, including King David, but she made no headway. Now they had a truce. Carlos stayed on his side of the street and she stayed on hers.

She smiled as she thought about him. In a harsh way, he was simply giving voice to the skepticism people had always expressed about her profession. "Do you really think you're some kind of fortune teller, astrologer, or soothsayer?" they would ask. The more aggressive ones would say, "Don't you just take advantage of people's narcissism?"

Her only rebuttal was to engage them in conversation, gently probing the details of their lives. If they were willing to share at a meaningful level, she would find it. She would see the beauty in their lives, the reasons—more numerous than they imagined—to be grateful, to seize each passing moment and savor it wholeheartedly.

Even as a child growing up in Reynosa, Mexico, her parents and friends had marveled at her temperament. "How can you always be so positive?" they said. Or "There's Alma. The world could be burning down around her, and she would see the splendor in the flames."

As she became conscious of her uniqueness, she realized she had an extraordinary gift. It was an unfailing optimism, an inner wellspring of hope, and its power filled her with joy and determination. By the time she was a teenager, people who had previously ridiculed her began to seek her counsel. They laid out their troubles with family members, love interests, or challenges at work, exposing emotional raw spots. She would help them discover a sense of peace, then encourage them with words that focused their blessings.

After her family moved to the U.S. and became citizens, she chose to cultivate her talent by attending classes on counseling and psychology at a local college. But clinical theories left her cold; they seemed divorced from the flesh and blood individuals she encountered in her daily life. Further, there were terms those theories rarely mentioned, especially the word love.

Love. She believed that giving and receiving it represented the highest calling for humanity. On this day, she would face her most difficult trial in practicing it.

At 10:00 a.m., her first appointment arrived, a woman named Vanessa. Her face was lined with the stresses of her busy schedule, juggling the pressures of parenting, marriage, and a law practice. She felt her life was slipping away, swallowed up by others who didn't appreciate her. She greeted Alma, then sat down on a couch across from her, checking her watch.

Same as every day, she said, "I'm afraid I don't have a full hour. I'm slammed. I've got an important deposition this morning."

Alma let her catch her breath, then said, "We'll make each moment count."

Vanessa smiled and relaxed a bit.

"It's hard to be someone who cares enough to give the fullness of their lives," said Alma. "Not everyone does that, Vanessa. Let's pick up where we ended last time. Tell me more about your parents. What were they like?"

"They were salt of the earth. Hardworking and responsible. I would even say they were selfless. But that's just the point. When I sat next to my father's bed during his final moments, I kept asking myself, 'Is this all there is?' Working yourself to the bone to provide for others, then dying in a hospital bed with tubes running out of your arms and nurses changing your catheter?'"

"Were you with him when he died?"

Tears welled at the corners of Vanessa's eyes. "Yes."

"Was he conscious?"

"Almost to the end. I'll never forget the last thing he said to me."

"What was it?"

Vanessa's tears flowed more heavily, and her chest seemed to spasm. She looked away, gathering herself. "He said, '*Mija*, you are a deep soul. I am so proud to call you my daughter.'"

With those words, Vanessa let out the depths of her grief, tears flowing freely in the sanctuary of Alma's studio. Alma said nothing, just reached across the table and gently laid her hand on Vanessa's. After a few moments, Vanessa looked up and gazed into Alma's eyes, her face vulnerable.

It was the moment Alma had been waiting for.

"Vanessa, you're an intelligent, capable, and powerful woman. You know that you can always choose to take more time for yourself. You can learn more about boundaries, making sure that others pick up their fair share of the load. I encourage you to do so. Meanwhile, I see *such* beauty in you and the memory you shared of your father. What a treasure to know that this man who poured out his life for his family felt a love for you that he could barely express. It's a blessing, an anointing, and please hear me when I say this. In a world where so many people are concerned primarily with their own selves and personal gain, you have discovered one of the deepest reasons we are created—to bring joy to others. This makes you a wealthy woman in the realm of the Spirit."

Vanessa lowered her gaze and took a deep breath, her hand squeezing Alma's in a gesture of gratitude.

Then there was the session with Victor at 1:00 p.m.

He entered the room with an air of confidence, an outer façade that he usually dropped when he was in Alma's presence. A recovering alcoholic with four years of sobriety under his belt, Victor managed a Tex-Mex restaurant and art gallery, often displaying his own photographs, including some that had gained national attention. He was a tall, handsome man with dark hair and full lips. The crow's feet around his lustrous brown eyes added character to his face, speaking of hard paths and difficult lessons.

Victor had a sponsor in AA, a man who helped him remember to *never* take another drink; it would only lead to blackouts, hangovers, and suicide by degrees. But the sponsor was rigid, even harsh, in applying Twelve Step principles. Alma knew that Victor came to her for a listening ear that was gentler and more affirming.

When he settled into his chair and greeted her, Alma noticed that he looked more haggard than usual.

"You're struggling with something."

"Yeah, I've been having trouble sleeping."

He rubbed one hand over his brow. "I know that regret is a waste of time. It's self-centered, what people in the program call stinking thinking. But at night I wake up and I can't go back to sleep. I get obsessed over the wreckage in my past. Images of people and situations swarm over me like mosquitoes. There must be more to sobriety than this…"

"That's true," said Alma.

"It *is*. And even though I don't have the urge to drink again—*honestly*—I know I must find a way to quit these thoughts and find some serenity. I just can't seem to get there."

"You're so hard on yourself."

Victor smiled with a tinge of sadness. "Self-criticism comes naturally to me," a dubious inheritance from my seriously fucked-up family."

Alma chuckled, then gently changed the subject.

"When those nighttime regrets come rushing at you, is there one memory in particular that's especially painful?"

She instantly hit a nerve.

"Yeah. My regrets over losing Mary Ann."

"Who was she?"

"A romance I enjoyed for a few years. We had this

amazing connection. Physically, intellectually, creatively. I sometimes feel that our time together, especially our lovemaking, spoiled me for anything in the future. It was that good..."

He drifted away for a second, wandering in a garden of memories.

Alma brought him back to the present. "What stings the most when you remember her?"

He looked at her, almost reluctantly. "I lost her because of my selfishness, this gnawing need for affirmation inside me. It's part of the pressure that has always triggered my drinking, and I directed towards her. She felt suffocated by my need for attention, I don't blame her, but when I think of losing her, a fissure of grief opens inside me. It's connected to all the other losses in my life. I don't know... it's hard to describe. It's like a wave of melancholy."

Alma let the wave roll over him for a moment.

"There are so many aspects of the Twelve Steps that I love," she said. "Especially their reminder that letting go of self-judgment is a daily reprieve, something we achieve through spiritual disciplines. With memories like that, I can understand your restlessness and stress in the middle of the night. But tell me, what are your waking hours like now compared to when you were drinking?"

He thought for a few seconds, his face brightening. "They are *so* much better. I'm getting more accomplished, and I'm doing it in a natural way. My business and art flow out of me rather than being forced. And I've finally begun to have a short time of meditation. I use my early morning walks to settle into a rhythm and listen to the sounds around me."

He looked up at her with a smile that was more peaceful. It was the moment she had been waiting for.

"I read devotional literature from many traditions," she said, "including the Hebrew Psalms. There's a verse in Psalm 84 that I love. 'Better is one day in your courts than a thousand elsewhere.' It tells me that when we begin to live in the center of each 24 hours, uplifted by the Presence that loves and affirms us, time expands dramatically. Psalm 84 uses the hyperbole of a 1,000:1 ratio just to drive home the point.

"I see such positive things happening in your life, Victor. The darkness of the past with its self-destructive behaviors is being replaced with the fullness of today. Your Higher Power is redeeming your time, and any regrets you have will eventually dissolve into the beauty of this new life, one day at a time. I am sure of this."

"I hope so," he said. "Thank you so much, Alma."

———

In the middle of the afternoon, Alma was going over some notes when she heard the bell ringing at her front door. She looked up to see a young man dressed in baggy jeans and a black tank top. His head was shaved, his arms sleeved with tattoos, including one that was all too familiar to her: the black and gold crown of the Latin Kings, one of the most vicious gangs in San Antonio. The Kings had an elaborate set of morals, beliefs, and rituals, and they claimed they had a wider responsibility to the Latnix community. Alma had often thought that their guidelines, if freed from violence, could truly make a difference to her people.

From the moment he entered, the young man's eyes locked on hers.

"Walk-ins welcome, *si*?" he said.

"Yes, they are," she said. "Have a seat."

He sat down, his eyes still fixed on hers, the rest of his face impassive.

"Can I help you?" she asked, trying to conceal her growing anxiety.

"I'm sure you can't. I'm here because *you* are the one who needs help. You need to free your mind, *mujer*."

She forced a smile and said, "I'm always open to new insights."

He laughed, a guttural sound that rolled across the table.

"That sounds like something you'd say."

"I'm serious," she said, not blinking.

"I'm sure you are, and that's the problem."

"What do you mean?"

"We'll get to that. But first, a question."

"Anything," she said.

"You're from the Fuentes family on Calaveras, aren't you?"

Her mind began to work, putting his question together with the gang tattoo on his forearm. She didn't like the way this conversation was turning.

"Yes," she answered. *"Ellos son mi familia."*

"Then you'll be happy to know that Bennie sends you his greetings. More than that. He asked me to give you a message."

At the mention of her nephew's name, something caught inside her chest and a vivid memory returned.

It was one of those endless days in late summer, heat and humidity lingering in the air. She was preparing dinner, looking out the open kitchen window at her husband, Beto, who was trimming roses in their front yard. The skyscrapers of San Antonio loomed in the distance. She breathed in the fragrance of jasmine that seeped through the screen.

Suddenly, she saw her sister-in-law rushing down the sidewalk, stopping to talk to Beto, clearly distraught. After a moment, the two of them turned towards the house and fixed their gazes on Alma. The anguish in their eyes was unmistakable.

Bennie had been arrested for murder, and all the fragmented pieces of his dark descent locked into place. Despite family support and professional counseling, he had drifted into the gang life that permeated so much of the West Side culture in San Antonio, recruited by the Latin Kings. His whole demeanor had changed, and no one, not even his closest family members, could convince him to change his direction.

Her sister-in-law gave them the gory details. Bennie had been ordered to warn away a rival gang member. What started as verbal threats escalated into violence until Bennie shot the other young man with his 9MM Glock in broad daylight outside a drug trafficking house. He would have escaped except for the bravery of a witness across the street, an old man who said he was "no longer going to surrender" to the intimidation that gang members used to quiet bystanders.

The old man's identification led to an arrest and conviction. On the day of judgment, with the court packed by the Fuentes clan, Bennie sat defiantly as he received a prison sentence of 20 years. Once behind bars, he made it clear that he didn't want family members to visit.

"What's wrong?" said the young gangster, jolting Alma from her memories. "Speechless?"

Alma quickly collected herself. "No. I just haven't heard Bennie's name for a while. How is he doing?"

"*El es un soldado fiel.* One of our most effective enforcers inside. When we need the hand of vengeance, he's more than willing."

The young man looked at Alma with a malignant smile, expecting a reaction.

"So, that's it?" she snapped. "You came here to share the sadness and tragedy of my nephew's life? Why would you do that?"

"Because Bennie said your outlook on the world needs correction, and I agree. I also have a family member who lives in a fog, *mi tia* who comes to see you. She wastes her social security money on your fucking insanity."

Alma suspected he was speaking of Elodia, one of her few clients from the old days, a widow battling depression and a growing fear of the violence in her neighborhood.

Partly from anger, partly because of her basic nature, Alma decided to commandeer the conversation, turning it in a different direction.

"*Bastante!* You delivered your message. Tell Bennie this the next time you see him. No matter how disturbed his life has become, no matter how far he has descended into darkness, there is *always* hope. No one is outside the influence of love, even the most hardened criminal."

The young man grew rigid as she spoke.

"Bennie knew you'd say something like that. But you're wrong, and here's the rest of his message. He told me to tell you that the world is *not* beautiful. It's full of violence and selfishness. It's full of inequality. Look at this city. So many of our people live in rundown *barrios,* struggling to get by. Their homes are sagging. Their schools are shabby and poorly funded. Then drive 10 miles north, *mama*, and see the suburbs. People live in big homes far away from our reality. They don't give a shit. They just want to get their piece, their portion. I don't blame them. In fact, I agree with them. Find a way to get what you deserve, by any means necessary."

"But the means don't always..." Alma tried to intervene.

"Shut up! Bennie and I aren't finished. We want you to remember the history of our people. Even you, with your idiotic optimism, can't deny the racism that has existed here since this land was seized from Mexico. It's the same oppression that affects people of color all over the world. It is *not* beautiful! You hear me? It's evil. For too many years it has told our children that they are somehow inferior, when really they are kings and queens!"

"But intolerance is not our basic nature," said Alma, raising her voice. "Inside each of us..."

The young man slammed his fist on the table. "You're no better than the oppressors," he hissed. "You fill people's minds with this narcotic of false hope. You keep them from joining the struggle, from demanding what is rightfully theirs!"

He suddenly stood, staring down at her, visibly calming his breath until he was preternaturally still. Alma felt a chill run through her body, as if a curtain of ice had dropped in her studio.

"OK, Beauty Seer," said the young man with a sneer. "That's all I have to say to you right now. But I'm *sure* we will meet again. Soon. You need additional correction. And you'd better stop seeing my aunt, Elodia."

Without another word, he turned and left the studio.

Alma was as shaken as that day she found out about Bennie. It wasn't so much the young man's words, or even the memory of her nephew. It was that final stillness, his complete immersion in the glacial ether of his dark world view. He was a true believer. She again felt a shiver run through her body.

The rest of the afternoon passed without incident, and she was able to maintain her composure despite traces of the young man's presence in her mind and heart. Her final appointment was late in the day, and by the time she locked the front door, dusk was settling over the city. She went to the rear of her studio to exit along the alley where she parked her car. She stepped out, turned to lock the bolt, then heard quick footsteps crunching in the gravel behind her. A rough hand grasped her around the neck and twisted her body against the wall of the building. She could feel its bricks radiating heat from the summer day.

She half-turned her head to see the young Latin King, a crazed look in his eyes, a smile like a grimace twisting his lips. He lifted a handgun and pointed it just inches from her skull.

"Stop struggling or I'll shoot you right now," he whispered harshly.

"You don't have to…" she said.

"Shut up," he commanded, his hand growing tighter around her throat.

She attempted to swivel her head, to see if there was anyone nearby who could help. A siren wailed from the heart of the city, then receded. The last light of day bathed the alley in shadows.

Using all her strength, she twisted until she was fully facing him, galvanizing her fear, looking beyond the barrel of the handgun to focus on his eyes.

"If you would only…" she started to say.

"What? If I would only *what*? Enough with your fucking bullshit! You're like a fortune cookie made in a Los Angeles sweat shop. People like you are hopelessly out of touch with reality."

"Reality depends entirely on how we…" she tried one more time.

"*Bastante*! Here's another lesson from Bennie and me. Think of it as a test. Maybe your *final* one. Look deeply into this gun. What beauty do you see in there?"

Alma focused on the black circle of the barrel, and it seemed to her like the void that opens in the lives of so many people, threatening to engulf them. The heart of darkness, the cistern of death, evil, and hopelessness.

Simultaneously, there was that answering fountain of her soul, rising with unquenchable power to fill her heart. It released her, bringing a smile to her lips. She looked beyond the gun, and her eyes bored into those of her attacker, no longer afraid, filled only with compassion.

"I see that even you, with all your anger, are a child of God."

The two of them remained frozen for a few seconds until the young man slowly lowered his gun.

The Sanctuary

Allan's routine was the same every morning. He left his downtown loft apartment and walked along the street to his favorite café for breakfast. Then he sat at his usual table and scrolled through news and stock market quotes on his laptop. Or he would pull up his Kindle app and read a wide variety of philosophy, poetry, and fiction. An anonymous man blending into the urban landscape, his body language saying, "Please leave me alone."

Along his route he passed some massive wooden doors—painted red, now faded—standing at the top of concrete steps blackened by moss. It was the entrance to a historic Protestant church, its founding members having bailed to the suburbs. The tall edifice and its spire seemed forlorn, tiredly keeping watch over a distant time and place, an anachronistic sentinel amidst the bustle of downtown.

One time he climbed the steps and tried the cold metal knobs on each door, but they were locked. A sign tucked under the eave said, "Office Around the Rear," so weathered that it belied any signs of life. *Typical,* he thought, *Inaccessible, irrelevant.*

After that day, he no longer focused on either the doors or the building. They were hidden in plain sight, like computer wallpaper he rarely noticed.

Then, one morning, a flash of color caught his peripheral vision. He looked up to find a bright banner hung above the church's portal. Characters Welcome, it proclaimed, and it made him chuckle. *At last, a little variety, some invention, a splash of color.*

The doors were slightly ajar, and through them came the sound of voices and laughter, like a golden stream of music spilling into the street.

He was tempted to investigate, but he kept pace toward the café.

The next day, buzzed on espresso, he passed the church again. The entrance was still ajar and the voices from inside beckoned him. With a mixture of curiosity and trepidation, he mounted the steps, pushed one of the doors open, and entered.

He found himself in a vaulted vestibule, its walls lined with historic photos from the church's storied past. The air smelled musty with a faint tinge of incense. The maroon carpet underfoot seemed new, a sign of recent remodeling. Ornate chandeliers twinkled above, their lights shimmering in the lofty space.

He heard the laughter again, coming from a room to the right. Feeling out of his element—not only in a church but making contact with strangers—he walked over and looked inside.

A dozen men and women of various ages were seated on chairs in a circle. They instantly turned towards him, their faces warm and welcoming.

"You found us!" said a man in his thirties, dressed in casual clothing, a purple beret jauntily perched on his head. "Have a seat if you'd like."

"No thanks," said Allan. "I'm just looking around. I've passed this church a thousand times but never came inside."

"We hear you," said an older woman from the other side of the circle. She wore a rainbow tie-dye shirt and turquoise parachute pants, dreadlocks piled on her head. "This place was cold and inhospitable for a long time, especially with its theology." She winked. "But there's hope for change everywhere, eh?"

Allan almost winked in return. Instead, he smiled and said, "Is this some kind of Bible study or discussion group?"

"More like a support group," said a young Black man with studs in his ears. He wore a stylish dark suit with a flamingo-colored shirt. "Sort of like Characters Anonymous, except we aren't so anonymous."

That drew laughter from the group.

"Are you sure you don't want to take a seat?" asked the man who had first spoken.

"Not right now. Sorry to interrupt you."

"No problem at all," said the woman with the dreadlocks. "Come back on Sunday and join us in the sanctuary."

There was a chorus of yeses and nodding heads.

"I'll think about it. Anyway, thanks again."

With his pulse elevated, his breathing shallow, Allan turned self-consciously and reentered the vestibule, struck again by its loftiness. He noticed another set of wooden doors tucked in the rear, even grander than those at the entrance. Hung above them was a sign with bold lettering that simply said, *The Sanctuary*.

His unease grew stronger, stoked by old memories. His father was agnostic, his mother a practicing Catholic, and because his dad reluctantly acquiesced, Allan's upbringing was plagued by forced church attendance and the brainwashing of a confirmation course. He'd expended a lot of energy to disengage from that web, and his separation grew wider as he observed true believers from many faiths, people convinced that their vision of God or Spirit or Higher Power was the path that everyone should take. He abhorred proselytizers of any stripe, giving them a wide berth.

Who are these people? Are they some kind of sect? They don't look like a normal church crowd. What would I find if I entered that sanctuary on a Sunday?

He shook his head with an emphatic no, then exited to the street.

Allan avoided the church for a week, changing his routine to walk on the opposite side of the street. But sheer force of habit was deep, and one day, lost in thought, he found himself on his usual route. His eyes returned to the banner once again, this time flapping in a summer breeze that gusted down the street.

He stopped at the bottom of the steps. The doors were still ajar and he heard distant conversation from inside. *Jeez, do they ever stop?*

Compelled again by curiosity, he walked up the steps, entered the vestibule, and went straight to the meeting room. The group was bigger this time, and they turned to him with hospitable smiles.

"Ahh, you're back," said the man who had greeted him initially. He now wore a beige beret. "There's a seat for you here," he said, gesturing to an empty chair on his right.

Allan smiled sheepishly, nodded, and sat in the circle. It felt like a tractor beam was drawing him to this time and place.

"No matter who you are or where your life's path has taken you, remember this," said the man in the beret. "In this circle, and hopefully someday in *all* the world, characters are welcome."

Members of the group nodded their heads and a couple of them murmured *Amen*.

Then, as if his entrance was a natural occurrence, the flow of conversation continued. The woman with piled dreadlocks, this time sporting a Death Cab for Cuties T-shirt, began speaking. She had a hard face with pronounced crow's feet around her dark blue eyes.

"Like I was saying, I endured that insanity in my hometown for *way* too many years. But I finally couldn't tolerate that unholy alliance between local churches and nationalism. I was chronically pissed off. Get this! During one of the elections, a neighbor down the street posted a campaign sign that read *God, Guns, and Country.* Can you fucking believe that? Can you imagine children passing that sign on their way to school? I left organized Christianity when I was a teenager, but even my basic knowledge of the Bible showed me that Jesus taught nonviolence. He would *never* bless 21st century militarism or underscore the Second Amendment!"

Allan found himself nodding along with others, grooving with the woman's grievance. It was like she was giving voice to his own sentiments.

"Anyway, I realize we're here to learn an appreciation for *all* types of characters, including those we disagree with. Even our enemies. I know I have judgment and anger issues to resolve. It's a character flaw and it plagues me. But back then I wasn't concerned with learning how to forgive or accept anyone. My remedy was to leave town and start hitchhiking west. I'm still not sure about some of the God talk y'all use, but I *do* feel that something guided my steps to this door. Especially into our sanctuary. I'm grateful for each of you. That's all I have to say today."

The group responded with soft clapping and a nodding of heads.

The young Black man Allan had noticed earlier began to speak. He had a handsome, gentle face, his eyebrows carefully plucked, his hair shorn close to his head.

"Thanks, Marla. You all know the piece of her story that intersects with my life. That weird, cultish variety of the Christian faith that has a history of homophobia. My husband, John, is still skeptical of my coming to a place of worship like this. He bears the scars of judgment inflicted on so many gay people over the years."

He paused and looked down at his silk shirt, picking at something on the collar. "Sometimes it's hard to really believe that the arc of history bends towards justice. But this group gives me hope that maybe it does. I keep inviting John to join us in the sanctuary, but he just shakes his head like he's waiting for me to come out of a trance."

He chuckled, then looked up, his eyes slowly circling the group. "Thanks for listening."

Soft applause, murmurs, then a silence that grew until it was pregnant. Allan was so accustomed to the hubbub of the city, that he found the lull nourishing. No one seemed in a rush to fill the vacuum until a short woman sitting directly across from him began to speak in a soft voice. She had a soft, slightly pudgy face, her hair cut short with bangs. She wore a gray sweatshirt and gray sweatpants, her legs tucked up underneath her on the chair.

"Thank you, Jody. I really hope we can meet John someday."

She glanced down at her lap, took a deep breath, then looked up again. "I've shared before about my battle with invisibility. Everywhere. In my family, at school, at work. It sounds like whining to say that people took me for granted, but they did. I blended into the background so quickly that others didn't pause enough to see me or listen to my uniqueness. I found the same thing in a church I attended in my previous city. The people were nice during worship, especially when they greeted me at the door, but afterwards during what they called their fellowship time, they clustered together and I often sat alone."

Her voice grew louder, more insistent, tinged with anger.

"To show you my poor self-esteem, I stayed at that church for years. I saw people who joined at the same time I did get chosen for leadership roles. Who's to say I'm not a leader? Who's to say that my years spent as an invisible woman don't give me a special level of empathy for the *very* people that *every* church should be reaching!"

She was almost shouting now, and the woman sitting next to her said, "You go, Amanda! *Practica tu grito!*"

The woman took Amanda's arm and the two leapt to their feet, letting loose a loud series of high-pitched yips. The rest of the group stood and yipped with them, everyone laughing and shuffling their feet. Allan was the only one sitting, but somehow he didn't feel embarrassed, just intrigued by the outburst.

When everyone was seated again, Amanda turned to the woman next to her and said, "Gracias, Yasmin! That made me feel like I was in the sanctuary on a Sunday!"

Yasmin gave Amanda a hug, then turned to the group. "You heard those cries. Those are the exultant voices within each of us. Our unique voices freed from the judgments and oppression of the world around us. *Viva el santuario!*"

Everyone clapped again. A young man with dark hair, dark eyes, an aquiline nose, and tattoos sleeving one of his arms, spoke next.

"Amanda, I had a different experience with church leadership. I got involved in a community of people who were much older than me, people steeped in their traditions. Some of those folks had been part of that church for decades.

I gave in to my grandmother's nonstop invitations, thinking I would never like it there. But the pastor had a captivating style of preaching. It was real and down-to-earth, sensitive to people seeking truth no matter their backgrounds. I had lunch with her, and she laid out her goals and frustrations in trying to revitalize that inner-city congregation. She was really trying to connect them to the streets. I loved her."

He paused, chuckled, then shook his head.

"I ended up joining. The older members were gracious, but I quickly saw that I represented a type. You know what I mean. A token young person with an alternative look. It made them feel more inclusive. Anyway, they invited me to join their committee of elders and I accepted. Man, it was *so* frustrating, like pushing the same rocks uphill over and over. Finally, both the pastor and I got the board to agree to open our building to the homeless for an evening. It was part of a citywide coalition of churches trying to practice hospitality."

He paused, shrugged his shoulders, and sighed. "I'll never forget that night. It was amazing. For me, it was a pivotal point to a new future. But at the elder's meeting the next week, the main topic of conversation was about the wear and tear on our carpeting if we continued inviting the homeless to stay. Jesus Christ, what can you say?"

He leaned back in his chair, obviously finished. An olive-skinned woman with almond-shaped eyes, dressed in white linen, raised her voice.

"It's always so interesting to hear your stories," she said, pushing a strand of dark hair behind her ear. "Until coming here, I had absolutely no experience with any kind of religion. My parents were loving people engaged in our community, but they were adamantly atheist. Not only because they believed that every god in history was a fabrication of human hopes and dreams, but also because of the atrocities and intolerance they had seen from believers of many faiths throughout the centuries."

She paused and slowly looked around the circle, opening her arms as if she were embracing them all. Then she laughed contagiously.

"But here I am," she said. "I am!'

"We are!" responded the group in unison.

───────────

To his great surprise, Allan changed his routine and began attending the group regularly. Its solid core of members always welcomed newcomers. Some stayed, some never showed again. For many sessions, Allan didn't say a word. They invited his input and when he declined, they simply smiled and nodded. They never pressured him, and though he didn't take part in the conversations, he always found them stirring on levels he thought had long been dormant in his life.

Finally, over a period of a few days, he episodically shared the highlights of his past: his upbringing in Massachusetts, the bipolar influences of his parents, his education in IT, his move to the West Coast, his stellar success with a Silicon Valley start-up that led to early financial freedom.

In the embracing atmosphere of the group, he became aware that he was whitewashing his life, so he gradually opened up more vulnerably. He revealed his battles with depression, the failure of his only marriage, his struggles to stay connected with his twin daughters, both of whom blamed his mood swings as the source of their family's failure. Then he admitted the most pressing issue that plagued him when he awoke at night, staring at the ceiling. His loneliness. Despite all his inner justifications that living alone was *just fine*, he hungered for companionship.

An odd thing happened as he divulged those raw details. He discovered a level of acceptance, a sort of unconditional love, that he had always dreamed of but never experienced, not even in his family of origin or his marriage. It was like knots unwinding deep within him, or an expanding of his chest that seemed to draw more oxygen.

Still, despite his growing comfort with the group, he rebuffed their repeated invitations to enter the sanctuary on a Sunday. He wasn't quite sure why. It was as if passing that threshold would be a complete capitulation to a new lifestyle, a new him, and he wasn't ready for that. It was an odd, defensive thought, but there it was.

One sunny summer Saturday, Allan was browsing the vendors at a downtown farmer's market when he heard a voice nearby.

"Hello, Allan."

He turned to find the almond-eyed woman smiling at him, whose name he now knew. She was dressed in jeans and a colorful blouse, her dark hair falling gracefully over her shoulders.

"Hello, Dona."

"Do you come here often?" she asked.

"Yes, my loft is only a block away and I love the freshness of this produce. I also like to sit over there and people watch."

He pointed to a row of concrete benches shaded by overhanging elms.

"Nice spot," she said. "I also like to people watch."

She paused, as if deciding whether to go further. "This may sound strange, but I've been experimenting with my perspective, especially in public places. When I watch, I try to observe how my mind responds. Am I reacting to people as types? You know, cataloging skin colors, body shapes, clothing choices, tones of voice. Or can I just see each person, really *see* them? Does that make sense?"

He smiled. "It does. It's hard, isn't it, to just be in the moment and let go of the constant chatter and judgments? I remember reading a powerful piece by Krishnamurti to that effect. The line I recall is this, 'The ability to observe without evaluating is the highest form of intelligence.'"

She smiled and studied him, putting her finger playfully to the side of her temple. "Hmmm, I see a tall man, clean shaven, a slightly bemused smile on his handsome face. His hair seems to have been cut by a stylist. Even his casual clothes are expensive. I might think lawyer or stockbroker, but not someone who delves into Krishnamurti."

He laughed. "Case in point about observing without evaluating, eh?"

She laughed in return, then lifted her tote filled with a colorful variety of vegetables. She reached inside it.

"Here," she said, handing him a large naval orange. "Just smell that."

He took it, lifted it to his nose, and inhaled its tangy aroma.

"My place is also nearby," she said. "Would you like to join me for some stir fry?"

He grinned and nodded. "That sounds nice."

Her loft was on the seventh floor of an old Art Deco building he had always admired. Her view of the city was stunning, and he noted the tastefulness of how she had decorated her space. It was maximalist, showcasing a profusion of pictures and mementos on every wall. Some were photos of exotic locales that featured her in the foreground. Others were artifacts he presumed were from those travels, including masks, draped cloth, bits of sculpture on small shelves. At first it seemed too busy, too complicated, but he quickly saw how it formed a colorful mosaic.

"Would you like a glass of wine?" she asked.

"I'd love one."

She retrieved a bottle of merlot from a cupboard, skillfully uncorked it, then poured two generous glasses. She lifted hers.

"Prost, salud, *gānbēi,*" she said with a laugh.

He laughed in return. "Santé!"

They clicked glasses and took long draughts. His eyes strayed to an antique bookcase against a wall to his right. As he scanned the titles, he noticed a wide assortment of poetry: Auden, Rilke, Plath, Eliot, Hughes (both Ted and Langston), Neruda, Oliver. He could scarcely take them all in.

"That's quite a library. It even surpasses mine."

"You're also a lover of verse?"

He nodded, his eyes still scanning the titles.

"I've been immersed in Rilke's *Book of Hours* lately," she said.

"I've only read a few scattered poems by him, and none in that collection. What's made you linger with him for so long?"

She smiled, obviously pleased to have the conversation. "This translation is called *Love Poems to God*. Almost every selection speaks to me. There's a particular poem where he laments that none of us live our true lives. We appear behind masks formed from segments of our experience, and our real selves never get exposed. He wonders if there's a storehouse somewhere, a repository for all these unlived lives, like dusty suits of armor or old clothes hanging limply."

She paused and looked out the window.

"Then he says that despite all of this he senses a mystery living in and through everything. In music, the wind, flowers and animals, human streets that wind through time. And he closes with these words I memorized, *"You, oh God? Is it you, God, who lives it?"*

She spoke the words as if each had its own gravity, an eternal life all its own, letting Rilke tattoo the words into his memory.

"That's beautiful," he said, "but why did it speak to you so deeply?"

She smiled and was silent for a bit, mulling her

response. "It describes how I felt about my life for so long. I played roles in my career, in my various friendships, even in my family. I've always valued transparency and intimacy with others, but there are such great divides between us when it comes to sharing our true selves. I came to believe that we are born alone and we die alone. That didn't depress me. It just caused me to keep a sober distance from others. It was like I was watching life from a slightly detached perspective. Does that make sense?"

"Completely. At some point in my own life, I resigned myself to living alone, especially after my divorce. Our breakup was amicable, but at the root of it was this realization that we never really understood each other. We were strangers under the same roof. That became a life lesson of its own."

"I hear you," she said. "I had a similar experience in my own marriage before it dissolved."

She paused, took another sip of wine, then looked out the window at the glittering lights of the city. "When I first read those poems from Rilke, it awakened me to an unconscious thought that must have been there all along. Something I had never voiced. Maybe there *is* One who knows me completely. Maybe it is the One so many people call God."

She laughed. "I was raised with parents who were atheists, so you must understand how alien that concept was to me. Still, it got hold of me and started to grow. I began to feel like there was a presence in me looking out at the world through my eyes. Not in a controlling way, but benign, even loving. A partner, if you will. I read some other words in

143

Hebrew scripture. Psalm 139. Are you familiar with that poem?"

"Somewhat. I've heard it read at memorial services. David's description of God's omnipresence, right?"

She nodded. "Yes. *O LORD, you have searched me and known me. You know when I sit down and when I rise up; you discern my thoughts from far away. You search out my path and my lying down and are acquainted with all my ways. Even before a word is on my tongue, O LORD, you know it completely.*"

"Beautiful in a way," he said, "but also kind of suffocating. It reminds me of the 'god as a meddling conscience' my mother always peddled. You know, constantly watching us to catalogue our sins. Still, I hear what you're getting at. David is a fascinating character in Israelite history, especially when you imagine his Psalms arising from the heart of a young shepherd in the fields. My favorite is Psalm 8. *When I look at your heavens, the work of your fingers, the moon and the stars that you have established; what are humans that you are mindful of them, mortals that you care for them?*"

"You continue to surprise me," she said, lifting her glass. "And I love surprises."

He clinked his glass against hers. "I could say you surprise me as well, but to be honest, you seemed exotic from the first moment I laid eyes on you. So, I'm curious. Did that new notion of a presence in your life take you to the steps of the church?"

"It did. When I saw that Characters Welcome banner, the words were like a declaration of reality. We are *all* characters in our own rights, and we long for a welcoming. We long for a homecoming. I've been going there ever since. And the experience that brought it all together was in the sanctuary."

The rest of the evening passed in a glow of wine, excellent food, and a level of conversation for which Allan had long been hungering. Afterwards, they moved to chairs that Dona had positioned to maximize their view of the city. The aroma of the delicious stir fry meal lingered in the air. They were quiet for a long time, letting a warm silence envelope them. The lights of the city were mesmerizing, an electric ocean teeming with human life.

Finally, he turned his head to look at her and saw that she had already fixed her gaze on him. Neither of them flinched, looking deeply into each other's eyes, their mutual attraction as strong as the warmth of the alcohol.

"Would you like to spend the night?" she asked. "We could sleep in my bed, or I can make up the couch for you."

He chuckled. "I hope I don't put a damper on this beginning, but let me start on the couch. I don't usually have this much wine, and I would rather be clearheaded in bed. Also, I'd prefer not to walk home in the dark."

"No problem at all. Let me get it ready for you."

As he fell asleep, city lights shifting over the ceiling, that Rilke verse that Dona had shared came to mind: *"You, oh God? Is it you, God, who lives it?"*

He smiled as he drifted into deep sleep and a vivid

dream.

He was standing under the vault of the church's vestibule, but when he looked up there was no ceiling or chandeliers, just a sweeping view of the Milky Way revolving slowly like Time's mandala. Multi-colored nebulae shone through the billions of stars, and there was music—light, syncopated, like bells or guitar harmonics, building to crescendos all around him. Music of the spheres.

Allan had always been self-conscious about dancing, never feeling coordinated enough, but under that sweep of heaven he had an overwhelming desire to move. He began to leap around the vestibule, defying gravity, making great arcs with his body, as nimble as Nureyev or Baryshnikov. Laughter like a warm stream gushed up from somewhere deep inside him, and when he turned he saw that the doors of the sanctuary were wide open. Through them poured that same music of the spheres drawing him forward. And as he gave into its magnetic attraction, he saw Dona standing at the door's threshold with a Mona Lisa smile and open arms.

When he woke up, he was still laughing. There was no other sound in the loft. Sunshine poured in through the picture windows and he could smell the rich aroma of coffee already brewed. On the table next to the sofa was an empty cup and a handwritten note.

"Happy Sunday morning! I thoroughly enjoyed our evening and I hope there are many more to come. After your cup of java, consider joining me in the sanctuary if you are up in time. We could go to lunch afterwards. The celebration starts at 11:00. I know you'll love it!"

This time, he was ready to accept the invitation.

For years afterward, sitting next to his partner, Dona, Allan would tell newcomers to the group about the Sunday he had first stepped across the threshold into the sanctuary. About why he returned every week.

"It wasn't just the vibrant and uplifting music. It wasn't just the message of our pastor—so relevant to the spiritual journeys of all of us. It wasn't even the heartfelt testimonies of some of our members woven into the service.

"No, it was that first impression of a community the likes of which I had never experienced. Such a diversity of people standing side by side, lifting their voices, their arms, their hearts, their minds! Young and old, every skin color and style of dress, all sexual orientations, people from the street alongside people from corporate offices. Veterans of the church with their arms around newcomers. I have never, let me repeat that, *never* experienced such a sense of unity among human beings.

"It brought to mind a passage from my time of studying the Bible in Catholic confirmation classes. It's from the Gospel of Luke, a vision the Israelites had about the end of time. '*People will come from east and west and north and south and will take their places at the feast in the kingdom of God.*'

"Yes, that's it! That first time in the sanctuary and ever since, I feel like I'm at a feast of love, and it's a glimpse of what we can be *now*, not just in the future. A beloved community!

"It's a glimpse of heaven on earth, and it fills my heart with hope."

Four Loko

Sunlight seeped through gaps in the window blinds, creating patterns on the ceiling. John imagined framing it in his viewfinder, adjusting the ISO, f-stop, and shutter speed...

"It's like they say," Martin's voice interrupted his reverie. "I just don't have any control."

John pulled his gaze back to the men seated around him. Martin was a likable guy, tall and thin, of White and Mexican heritage, his long hair in a ponytail, his skin slightly oily. He was also a nonstop talker, irritatingly glib, and John was tired of his stories. Hell, John was weary of his *own* stories, but support group attendance was mandatory, whether you were private pay, Medicaid, or someone like John who'd been sentenced through the legal system. The goal was to get your ticket punched even if none of the therapy stuck.

And John *needed* his ticket punched. After his third

DWI, this one without a license, he'd been lucky to avoid extended prison time under strict Texas laws. His public defender was surprisingly effective, showing the judge how John's arrests had happened under 10 miles per hour in a few block radius, a befuddled drunk cruising slowly through Corpus Christi's North Beach. No accidents, no high-speed chase scenes, no damage done to people or property.

"Drunk driving is inexcusable," said the attorney, giving John a stern glance in the courtroom, "but my client has never had the benefit of rehabilitation. We ask that you give him that chance in lieu of incarceration."

Since the Nueces County Jail was crammed with serious offenders, the judge relented. John got 10 days in lock up, a $20,000 fine, two years' probation, continued suspension of his license, and assignment to a 60-day rehab program. If he finished his treatment without incident, he could piece together what was left of his life. If he failed, he faced years behind bars.

"I go into the 7-Eleven," Martin continued, "and I see a Four Loko sitting on the shelf in the cooler. Don't ask me why I like that sugary shit, but the alcohol content is dope. I say to myself, 'Martin, if you buy one of those, you'll end up in the drunk tank, and who knows where after that. Don't do it!' Then I open the cooler door, grab one, and head to the cashier."

One of the other group members, a muscular Army veteran named Jake, nodded his shaved head. "Yep, we're powerless."

"I hate that fucking word," blurted William, a private pay patient trying to save his job with an employer sympathetic to rehab.

"What word?" asked Jake. He knew the answer, but his own anger simmered just below the surface, tied to his tours in Afghanistan. He enjoyed goading people, especially William.

"Powerless. *That* word," said William. "And then we have to read that idiotic chapter in the AA Big Book that says, 'we are like men who have lost their legs, they never grow new ones.'"

William was a good-looking, impeccably dressed Black man, and he stretched out his long legs in front of him, his overpriced Nikes part of his drip.

"My legs are just fine," he said, controlling his tone to show that Jake wasn't riling him. "They're going to walk me right out of this shithole, and I'll never look back."

"Maybe," said Jake, not letting it go. "But they walked you straight in here to begin with, so maybe you don't have as much control as you think."

And so it went, back and forth, the eight of them corralled in a small room, one of three meetings per day. John sometimes found it helpful, but mostly he tuned out, thinking about his release slated for two weeks away. Thinking also about Angie and the thirst that prowled on the edge of his consciousness, as if it, too, was waiting for his discharge.

———

The staff at the rehab center called it a running track—a dirt path, roughly oval-shaped, carved behind the main buildings, surrounded by fences topped with concertina wire. John was one of the few patients who used it daily. It gave him a break from the claustrophobia of the meeting rooms and the constant chatter of others, but it didn't afford much relief from the weight of his predicament.

On a balmy afternoon four days before freedom, John walked the circle. Wind gusted from the north, laden with the sulfurous smell of nearby gas refineries. He fell into his usual stride, reliving the choices that had brought him to this place in time.

Born and raised in Corpus Christi, a graduate of Flour Bluff High School, he blended into the scenery— medium height, sandy brown hair, pleasant features, not especially talented in academics or sports, so unassuming that his peers left him alone with his thoughts.

What they missed was the richness of a mind that saw the world in all its patterns and hues. It was a gift that came naturally to John. He would look around him and see what others so often missed. The subtle interplay of colors undulating on waves around the Corpus Christi Marina. The contrast of light and shadow in downtown alleyways. Iridescence on the feathers of grackles, or the mysterious depths in the eyes of a cat. That moment when the evening clouds perfectly aligned with the horizon for a panoramic sunset, sailboats and tankers silhouetted in the foreground.

Fortunately, he had a teacher who recognized his artistic temperament and encouraged him to pursue it. John chose photography as his medium, and he eventually attended Texas A&M University, Corpus Christi. His father ran a successful plumbing business, expecting to turn over the reins to his only son. The notion of studying art mystified him, but he was also relieved that his boy had found direction after such an awkward adolescence, so he willingly paid the tuition.

John did well in his studies, even scoring a single-person exhibition at a local gallery during his senior year. In a short review buried in the Sunday edition of the Corpus Christi Caller Times, an art critic said, "John Kempton has a keen eye that lays bare the underlying beauty of our world."

After graduation, he got a job in that same gallery, but behind the scenes he'd begun to develop a serious drinking problem. His tolerance progressed quickly, moving from a couple beers, to six packs, to hard liquor. His boss at the gallery noticed his hangovers on multiple occasions, then finally let him go with the admonishment to get help.

He found a job as front desk clerk at a rundown North Beach hotel, where the owner let him rent a room that was out of commission due to its disrepair. That's when he struck up a relationship with Angie, one of the maids, a Latina slightly older than him who also liked to drink. She had lustrous eyes, long black hair, and a vivacious personality. She was quick to laugh, never complaining about her menial labor. They would get off their shifts, grab some drinks, then retire to his room. Angie had little formal education, but her intuitive grasp of people and situations fascinated John, as did her sense of humor, which lifted his spirits. Their time together was marinated in booze, but John felt a genuine affection for her, maybe even the seeds of love, and he believed she felt the same.

His DUIs, strung out over five years, occurred while driving the short distance to the liquor store for supplies.

The alcohol—like an evil twin—always told him that a few blocks of driving would be manageable. They weren't, and the wily cops seemed to hide their cars in different locations. The third arrest was by the same officer who'd busted him once before. As he placed handcuffs on John, he said, "Man, you must have a *very* thick skull."

John's father felt the same. He kept asking, "What triggers you? What's causing this?" John replied with a statement he adopted from one of the groups he'd attended after his first offense. "There's no trigger, Dad. I drink when I'm sad, when I'm happy, when I'm stressed, when I'm peaceful. I drink because I have a disease and I don't expect you to understand." His father would wince, shake his head, and turn away.

But honestly, John knew there *was* a trigger. The alcohol filled an aching emptiness, a void that came over him like a dark shroud, causing him to feel that nothing was more important than anything else. Relationships, activities, even his art, all drained of vitality in a gray landscape. It wasn't until this stint in rehab that they formally diagnosed his depression and offered a drug to mitigate it. He hoped it would help because, when it came to his drinking, it was exactly as Martin had said. No real control, and every hangover left him ashamed and more depressed, a toxic feeling he felt compelled to numb. It was a vicious downward cycle, an unstrung elevator plummeting to Hades.

Now, he was four days away from a new start. As he plodded around the track and his ring of karma, the sound of crunching footsteps snapped him from his thoughts. He glanced to his right and saw Martin coming alongside him.

"Man, do you always walk this fast?" Martin asked, breathing heavily, obviously out of shape.

"It's my natural rhythm."

"Well, slow down a bit. I want to show you something."

John cringed inside and adjusted his pace. Martin's company wasn't what he wanted at this moment. Martin reached into the pocket of his baggy jeans and pulled out a couple shot-sized plastic bottles of cheap vodka. He held them in his open palm like pearls of great price. John turned his head away, sighed, then looked back at Martin with exasperation.

"What the hell? How did you smuggle those in here?"

"My girlfriend, Darla. She has experience in that department. I can get as many as you'd like."

"Then what happens if they do a random piss test? What if you get busted?"

"I'm already at the bottom, man. What are they going to do with me?"

John shook his head. "Listen, Martin. For some strange reason, I like you."

Martin actually giggled.

"But I don't want any of your contraband. And don't take this the wrong way, but could you just leave? I like to have alone time on the track. It's my only place to get my thoughts together. Maybe even get my life together. Not to keep drinking. I'm only 32 years old and I still have time to get this right. *Entiendes*, amigo?"

Martin's expression sank, but he nodded his head.

"I hear you, bro. Enjoy your exercise." Then he turned back towards the rear entrance of the facility.

John calmed his irritation and walked for another half-hour, trying to stay in the present rather than obsess about the past. He halted as an image on the other side of the fence caught his attention. Five seagulls were perched atop a building. An American flag from an adjacent structure fluttered behind them, and in the distance rose a mountain of towering clouds. The lighting was perfect, the birds' heads tilted in different ways, as if they were engaged in conversation. He framed the picture in his mind, imagining the ISO, the f-stop, and the shutter speed, clicking it into his memory.

Then he thought about his camera equipment stored in his apartment, where Angie was staying until his release.

He also thought about the thirst still prowling there like a tiger.

They released John on a Wednesday afternoon, ordering him to check in with his probation officer two days later. His therapist offered some parting words. "I've seen your photos, John. You have real talent. I mean it. Don't get pulled down again. Use the tools you've learned. Go to meetings. Reach out to other alcoholics when you're tempted. And don't forget, your disease is doing pushups in the dark, ready to pounce if you forget to work your program."

John nodded, gave the guy a hug, then walked into the light of a beautiful day on the Texas Gulf Coast. The air was tinged with the smell of ocean brine, and a circus of white clouds paraded slowly overhead. He took a deep lungful and squared his shoulders. Angie was waiting for him in the parking lot, leaning against the rear of his beat-up Toyota Corolla. She looked luminous, her skin golden brown, her eyes bright, her hair pulled back with a bandanna.

She embraced him and kissed him on the cheek.

"*Felicidades, mi amor*. You graduated! It's good to have you back."

Angie drove them towards home, but just before getting on the Harbor Bridge, she pulled into a 7-Eleven. She reached into her purse, grabbed a twenty-dollar bill, and handed it to him.

"Will you get me one of my vape pods?" she asked, then added, "and maybe something for later so we can celebrate your freedom."

He looked at her, trying to gauge if she was serious, and the look in her eyes only puzzled him.

Inside the store, John made his way past the tall drink coolers, pausing to look inside. There was a row of colorful Four Loko cans. He immediately thought of Martin, then the other men in his support group. He thought of the legions of the addicted who find their way into rehab centers around the world, some trapped in revolving doors that slowly wind down to death. But also the others who find the miracle of new life.

A wave of emotion welled up inside him, a deep compassion for *all* of them, including himself. He remembered something his counselor had said.

"John, shame is one of the deepest aspects of this disease. Just remember that you are loved. Not only by whatever higher power you believe in, but by all those who have walked alongside you in your struggles. Forgive yourself. Be good to yourself."

John made the purchase and returned to the car, feeling comfortable inside his own skin as he swung into the passenger seat and handed Angie her pod.

"Nothing else?" she asked.

"Nope, that's it."

She smiled broadly, nodded, and steered the car back onto the street. With her left hand on the steering wheel, she reached over her right hand and placed it on his thigh, giving it a light squeeze. He gently returned the gesture.

As they passed over the Harbor Bridge, he looked down at familiar landmarks—the Texas State Aquarium, the shipping channel, and the USS Lexington in the distance. Sunlight bejeweled the water, fracturing into patterns that delighted him. A colossal freight ship was plowing towards the open waters of the Gulf, scattering the light like millions of tiny fish.

And he knew, right then, in his heart of hearts, that his own journey was headed for new ports, new adventures. Was it just a fleeting intuition? Was it just for today? Wasn't today all he really had?

He smiled and framed the ship against the glittering ocean, imagining the ISO, the f-stop, and the shutter speed, clicking it into his memory forever.

Baby Bridget's Ashes

Adrian Reynosa awaited his final appointment of the day. He was weary of urine tests, paperwork, and perfunctory questions with equally perfunctory answers. Some of his clients showed signs of improvement, but in the hollow words and shifty expressions of others he anticipated future incarceration. Sociopathy so often defied change.

After twenty years as a probation officer, he knew his perspective had grown cynical. Honestly, he didn't know how to recover that original spark of idealism that made him want to help men and women often ground underfoot by the system. His *abuela* kept working on him to come to church with her. *Have you talked to your cousin Eddie?* she'd ask. *Tienes que reencontrarte con tu fe, mijo.* Adrian deflected her questions, knowing that her ironclad religion couldn't accommodate his stark existential credo. He had no faith in a conventional sense, but his beliefs had always given him a sense of purpose. At least, until lately. So now, with increasing tinges of sadness, he would smile, gently shake his head, kiss her cheek, and say, *Te amo, abuela.*

He took a sip of tepid coffee, dregs from the last pot in the break room. The probation office was in a strip mall on the edge of the city's industrial zone. It featured a beauty salon, a taqueria, and a cellphone outlet. A couple of shops were vacant, routinely targeted by vandals who broke their windows or sprayed graffiti on their doors. The theory behind this satellite location was to be closer to the people, part of their low-income neighborhood. A version of community policing. Adrian thought it was a misguided notion, more hassle than help.

Through his office window, he saw Sylvia approaching. She was walking instead of riding her bike, carrying a plastic shopping bag in her hand. The late afternoon sunlight of a glorious spring day gilded her hair. She looked far healthier than when they had first met following her second bust for heroin possession. The court had sentenced her to mandatory rehab with a year's probation, and the treatment seemed to have stuck, at least for now. Her Twelve Step talk and her relationship to her sponsor had the ring of sincerity.

She knocked on his door.

"Come on in," he said.

She flounced in and flopped into the vacant chair across from his desk, setting the plastic bag on the floor. The scent of patchouli oil trailed into the room with her. Only 28 years old, her eyes still had a youthful vitality, but the creases around them spoke of a hard history.

"You look energetic," he said. "How are you feeling?"

"Today's a good day. My shift at the motel was light, and I caught a meeting during my lunch break."

"Any wisdom from the others?"

"Yeah, definitely. The topic was about the uselessness of regret. I needed that. I have this sick habit of looking backward and seeing how my addiction robbed me of so many things. Jobs, opportunities to get some schooling, healthy relationships. I don't know if *anyone* in my family will ever trust me again."

Sylvia grew up in a solid middle-class home. Her brother and sister had chosen the path of the American Dream, going on to college, careers, and families of their own. Sylvia, plagued with a disease none of her relatives could fathom, chose to drop out and make a mess of her existence, drifting between cities, jobs, men, and finally, homeless shelters. She was lucky to be alive, a blessing she now seemed to appreciate.

"You know the drill," said Adrian. "It doesn't matter if they ever understand you or this disease. You're not doing this for them."

"I know, I know," she said, showing a flash of her old rebelliousness. "Haven't you ever longed for the acceptance of another person?"

He immediately thought of his father, an intelligent and creative man, a teacher by profession, who nonetheless remained mired in machismo, emotionally mute for the duration of his life. Adrian's mother had escaped through divorce, her only contact being a bouquet of flowers she sent to her ex-husband's funeral. But healthy boundaries had been harder to maintain for Adrian, especially since he craved his dad's unconditional love.

"Of course I have," he said. "I'm just reminding both of us that some people will *always* withhold their approval. We need to know when to let go."

She rolled her eyes and shook her head. "Yeah, yeah. Let go and let God, like that irritating sign on the wall at my meetings. Just give me the kit."

From a box behind him, he removed a plastic bag that contained a specimen cup and a 10-panel test strip that would detect marijuana, cocaine, PCP, amphetamines, opiates, barbiturates, benzodiazepines, methadone, Quaaludes and propoxyphene. When he handed the cup to her, she snatched it impatiently.

She got up, went to a restroom across the hall, then returned with her specimen in hand. He set it in a black plastic box on a stand near the wall, then dipped in the stick and found it negative on all counts. Not surprising. After 20 years in this line of work, he had a sixth sense when someone was using again. Sylvia was clean.

"Only two months left," he said. "I'm proud of the progress you've made."

Her expression relaxed. "Thank you. Sorry about getting bitchy for a second. I'm still a work in progress."

He smiled tiredly. "I understand. We *all* have our rough edges. Just remember that your defiance is a trigger that could crush everything you've been building."

She looked down at her lap. "I know. My sponsor says the same thing." She sighed. "Anyway, I brought something I want to show you."

She reached into the plastic bag and removed a small cardboard box about 4 inches by 4 inches and slid it across the desk to him. It was slightly yellowed, secured by frayed plastic tape, and there was a label with spots of water damage affixed to its top. It read: "Identification Number 7592. Cremated remains of Baby Bridget Spell. Date of Birth, 9-10-1988. Date of death, 9-20-1988." Beneath that was the name of a memorial park in the city, Harris and Sons, a place Adrian was familiar with.

"What the hell?" he said with a bit of shock.

"I know. That was exactly my reaction when I first saw it."

"How did you end up with a box holding a baby's ashes from 34 years ago?"

"There was this middle-aged woman in the noon meeting a couple days ago. She claimed to have had a relapse after 20 years of being clean. She was over the worst of her withdrawal, but I could see she was still suffering. Something in her story touched me. It was like a warning sign flashing from the future, reminding me of what could happen if I let down my guard. When I found out she had no place to stay, I told her she could crash at my apartment."

"Sylvia…"

"I know, and I paid the price. When I got up this morning, my favorite backpack and my bike were missing."

"You're lucky that was all."

"Listen," she said with sudden firmness, "I'm not going to say, 'once a junkie always a junkie.' I ripped off my own share of people and look at me now."

"Fair enough, but what about these ashes?"

"Shit, I don't know. I found them on my kitchen counter when I woke up."

Adrian studied the box. He'd had a lot of strange experiences in his career; this was one of the weirdest. "Did you catch the woman's name?"

"I'm sorry, she mentioned it in the meeting, but I forget. I think it started with a C. She had blonde hair streaked with gray and pulled back in a ponytail. Her clothes were wrinkled but not dirty. She was nice enough even though she was mostly quiet and withdrawn. She did say that she had grown up here many years ago, but that was about all the info I could get. I did most of the talking. I *do* like to talk."

Adrian picked up the box, turning it slowly in his hand, reading the label again as if he might discover something new.

"So why did you bring it here?"

"I want you to take it."

"No way," he replied firmly. "What am I supposed to do with it?"

"I don't know. But please, will you take it? It creeps me out."

Sylvia's eyes seemed genuinely nervous.

"Alright," said Adrian with a sigh, taking the box and slipping it into the top drawer of his desk. "As a favor to you, I'll see if I can get to the bottom of this."

"Thank you," she said, already standing, anxious to go. "Same time next week?"

Adrian nodded and made a gently dismissive wave

of his hand.

"Yes, Sylvia. Same time next week. *Buena suerte.*"

———————

Adrian opened the door to his Spanish-style bungalow, kicked off his shoes, and went into the kitchen. After placing the plastic bag with the ashes on the counter, he snagged a Modela Negra from the refrigerator. His long-time girlfriend, Adela, was visiting her family in Monterrey, Mexico, so the house was quiet—only the distant white noise of the freeway six blocks away, a sonic background he normally didn't notice. He enjoyed his time alone, but he also missed Adela's warm *abrazos y besos* at the end of the day.

He pulled out a Tupperware container of *pollo y calabaza* Adela had prepared before leaving, stuck it in the microwave, then took the plastic bag with him into the living room. He sat down on the couch, opened the sack, withdrew the small cardboard box and placed it on the low-lying coffee table, staring at it as if willing it to speak. A verse from Neil Young's *Rockin' in the Free World* ran perversely through his mind: "There's one more kid that will never go to school, never get to fall in love, never get to be cool."

"Who are you, Bridget?" he said aloud. "Only ten days. How did you die? Where are your people? What can you tell me from beyond the grave?"

In the stillness of the house, he unexpectedly felt a tear run down his cheek. He had grown accustomed to loss, disappointment, and tragedy in the lives of his clients. The seamy and desperate sides of life were all too familiar to him, held at arm's length for his own peace of mind.

So why do these ashes affect me so deeply? he thought.

He ate his meal, had another beer to calm his restlessness, then streamed a crime series on Hulu until he was tired enough to crawl into bed. He could smell Adela's perfume on the pillows. Sleep came fitfully, interrupted too soon by the old recurring dream, the one his therapist said would likely decrease in frequency but maybe never disappear.

The scene was always the same, the epicenter of trauma that had changed him and his *primo* forever. Driving his modified Impala, its upscaled pipes rumbling beneath the floorboard, twilit scenes of their city flashing by outside. Eddie in the passenger seat, his window open, laughing as warm night air streamed over his face. Then, suddenly, the car of a rival gang careening around the corner, an escalating feud of senseless retaliation. The other car gaining, reaching Eddie's side, the shotgun blast like a metallic roar, Eddie slumping into the seat covered in blood...

The dream always ended there, as if the trauma of those fearful hours that followed—Eddie's life hanging in the balance—were too much to relive. Adrian sat up in his bed, reoriented himself, then glanced at the small box of ashes he had placed on his nightstand.

A plan for the next day took shape in his mind.

―――――――――

In the morning, after coffee and breakfast tacos, Adrian

called his office to speak with Angela, the clerk and scheduler.

"Hey Angie. Sorry for the hassle, but I won't be in today. Could you call my clients and reschedule? Something came up in a meeting with Sylvia that I need to track down. Sorry again. You're the best. I owe you a *carnitas* lunch plate from Nuevo Jalisco."

"Promises, promises. See you when we see you."

He disconnected then looked at the clock. Too early to start his investigation, so he changed into workout clothes and mounted the Peloton bike in his study, a luxury he had given himself for health reasons. He chose the half hour Power Zone Endurance ride, a lithe female instructor challenging him to dig deeply until his body was streaming with sweat. Then he showered, dressed, and returned to the living room with his cell phone.

At 9:00 a.m. sharp, he made his first call to the mortuary listed on the box. After navigating a labyrinthine set of numerical options, he finally got a live person.

"Harris and Sons," said a woman's voice, "where you are *always* part of the family. May I help you?"

"Yes. I'm a probation officer and one of my clients came into possession of a box of ashes cremated at your facility in 1988. I know that's a long time ago, but I'm trying to track down the family."

There was a long pause on the other end. "I see. Let me connect you with our director."

Adrian listened through a series of clicks until a man with a husky voice spoke. "May I help you?"

"I hope so. I have a strange situation here. I'm a

probation officer with the county and one of my clients brought a small box of cremains to my office yesterday. She said another woman left them with her. I'm trying to locate the baby's family if they are still around."

There was another long pause. "Does the box have any info on it?"

"It does," said Adrian, giving him the ID number, Bridget's name, the dates of her birth and death.

"Can I put you on hold for a few moments?"

"Of course. I appreciate your help."

The ensuing Muzak made Adrian chuckle, a completely inane version of Jimi Hendrix's *Little Wing*. Just as it ended, the man returned to the line.

"When you gave me the dates, I was afraid of this. Before we digitized our records twenty years ago, we kept some of the files in an underground basement. During a torrential rain, that room had flood damage, and we lost a whole section of paperwork. This would be one of those lost records. I'm so sorry."

"That's a real shame," said Adrian, feeling frustrated and annoyed.

"It is. Understandably, we had waves of complaints and some lawsuits. Our company barely survived it."

Adrian cleared his throat, surprised by the possessive sense of anger he felt over this small remembrance of a child. "Okay. Thanks for your time."

He abruptly ended the call, then began to implement step two of his plan. He opened his laptop, logged on, then started an online search for the name Spell with an app he used at work. There were four in the city, and though he realized it was a long shot, he wrote down the telephone numbers.

The first number was out of service, the second a voicemail greeting from a young woman. The third call rang so many times that Adrian was about to disconnect when suddenly the line clicked to life.

"Hello," said a man's voice inflected by old age.

"Yes, hello," said Adrian. "I'm sorry to bother you, but is this George Spell?"

"It is. Who are you?"

"My name is Adrian Reynosa. I'm a probation officer with the county, badge number 6667, and I've come across something I would like to speak to you about."

The line went silent for a few seconds. "I can't imagine why a probation officer would be calling me, but go ahead."

"Sir, I could tell you about it, but it would be far better for you to see something in person. First, though, let me ask you, do you have a daughter?"

There was another pause, longer this time.

"That question makes my head swim," said the old man. "The short answer is yes, my daughter may still be alive. Is this some kind of scam?"

"Not at all. It's just that, like I say, there's something I'd like to show you in person."

Adrian could hear the man's labored breathing.

"I'll give you my address, but I'm keeping the glass door locked until you show me both your badge and this item you seem so riled about. If you don't comply quickly, I will have my phone in hand to dial 911."

"That works," said Adrian, writing down the address and tucking it into his shirt pocket.

———————

George Spell's home was in a neighborhood of modest ranch houses on the northern edge of the city, a tract from the mid-60s. Most were well-maintained, with an occasional outlier in need of paint. George's fit the latter variety. While other yards were beginning to bloom with spring color, his was overgrown and gray, featuring an untrimmed oak tree and a cement bird feeder filled with dust and leaves.

Adrian walked up the front steps and knocked solidly on the outer glass door. There was no response. He tried again, a little firmer. Finally, he heard a shuffling noise growing closer until the inner door opened.

George was tall and lean, with a gaunt face and unkempt gray hair combed over his bald pate. He wore a blue bathrobe and walked with a cane. Despite his elderly appearance, his gaze when he looked at Adrian was strong and penetrating.

"Show me your ID," he said, his deep voice surprisingly forceful through the barrier.

Adrian held it against the glass. George looked it over.

"And the other item you mentioned?"

Adrian pressed the small box of ashes, label side forward, against the pane. As George glanced at it, straining to focus the words, his face slumped. He looked down and slowly shook his head, moving his cane across the floor as if writing a cursive message on the tile. Finally, he looked back at Adrian and shrugged his shoulders.

"I guess you better come in."

He led Adrian into a clean and comfortable living room that belied the house's shabby exterior. The air smelled faintly of cooking grease. George settled onto the couch slowly, seemingly in pain, then motioned for Adrian to sit in an easy chair to his right.

"You'd think," said George, "that after a career of walking multiple miles every day as a mail carrier, I would have some level of fitness in my so-called golden years. Just the opposite. Both knees replaced and arthritis in my back. I know you've heard it before, young man, but getting old is not for the faint of heart."

He straightened himself as if resurrecting his dignity. "Now, how the hell did you end up with a box of cremains that probably belong to a granddaughter I never held in my arms?"

"One of my clients brought them to my office yesterday. She allowed a woman from her Twelve Step group to spend the night, but in the morning she discovered that the woman had stolen her bike and backpack and left this box on the counter."

Adrian paused, then added, "What do you mean by *probably belong to*?"

George put one hand to his forehead, rubbing the wrinkles as if trying to erase them. "I say that because I haven't seen my daughter for over 30 years. I'm sure in your line of work you meet many people addicted to drugs and alcohol. When it's someone you love dearly, it can almost kill you. They call it codependency, but in my mind

171

it's just the logical steps any parent will take with a child who seems to be destroying herself. My wife Emily and I tried everything. Everything! But Carrie finally left and ended up on the street. She was in her early twenties at the time, pregnant from a man we never met, and I haven't seen her since."

Adrian's ears perked up. Carrie, a name that began with C. George picked up the box of ashes from the coffee table where Adrian had placed it.

"That was 1988," he said. "The same year listed on this box." He dug his hand more firmly into his brow. "Does your client know where the woman went? Does she know where she's living?"

"No. It's a mystery."

"I'm not surprised. In the end, we could never keep track of her. I'm certain that the all the pain from those years is what contributed to Emily's early death."

He brought the box closer to his eyes, shaking it as if to confirm the contents within. "Ten days. Ten measly days to spend on this beautiful broken Earth."

His chest suddenly convulsed as a guttural animal noise erupted from his throat, followed by tears running down his wrinkled cheeks and onto his bathrobe. He hung his head as if slightly in shame and started to sob. Adrian felt uncomfortable at first but then reached across and put his hand on the old man's shoulder. They sat like that for a few moments as Adrian lifted his eyes to a photograph on the wall. It was a happy scene—a couple in their late 30s or early 40s standing next to a beautiful teenage girl. Her long hair fell past her shoulders and her smile and eyes seemed to mischievously engage the photographer. They were standing on the edge of the lake at the local county park, a popular place for swimming and family picnics, its short pier extending into the background.

George finally stopped crying and collected himself. "Young man, I obviously have some painfully mixed feelings about you bringing this to me after all these years. Is it always better to know the truth? I'm not so sure."

His face took on a look of resolve. "Listen, I'm in no shape to deal with this. Will you do me a favor and find some way to properly bury or scatter these ashes? Something dignified?"

Adrian had hoped that George would ask him that question. "I certainly will, sir, and I'll let you know so you can be there if possible."

Adrian pushed open the door of Set Free Ministries, entered the lobby, then made his way down the hallway toward Eddie's office.

There had been no question about who he would contact next. The night of violence that changed their lives had set them on separate courses, but Adrian's deep ties to his cousin would never fade. Both had eventually gotten out of gang life. Eddie had a Christian conversion experience and started an outreach program that specialized in reaching young people on the streets susceptible to gang recruitment. Adrian had taken a path of servitude as well, but didn't share his cousin's faith.

After many fruitless theological arguments, mostly

about the presence of evil in a world supposedly overseen by a benevolent deity, the two of them had come to a truce. Eddie prayed for his cousin daily, but he accepted Adrian's reluctance to embrace a personal deity. Adrian saw Eddie's deep devotion, an inner wellspring that informed all his decisions, admiring his cousin's certainty without judgment. They didn't try to convert each other's worldviews but simply treasured the bonds of their blood relationship.

Eddie was seated at his desk, and when he looked up, Adrian had the same reaction he always had. Eddie's face, still so handsome in its upper reaches was disfigured below by the shotgun blast. It reminded him of a Roman bust he had seen in the antiquities section of the county art museum. A patrician face with the chin chipped away as if by the hammer of death and age. Eddie lit up when he saw Adrian.

"*Primo*," he said, then moved towards Adrian. They embraced warmly.

"Man, I can't remember the last time I saw you under this roof. To what do I owe the pleasure?"

Adrian sat down across from Eddie, took the box of ashes out of the plastic bag, then told his cousin all that had happened in the last 24 hours. Eddie listened intently without interruption.

"Can you help me?" Adrian said in closing. "I've been to a lot of the memorial services you've conducted, and you always find the right words. Also, maybe you can gather some of your members to attend. I'll ask Sylvia and see if she can muster a few from her recovery group. I was thinking we could do it down at the shore of the county lake

I saw in the Spell family picture."

Eddie picked up the box and cradled it in his palm reflectively. "There's a lot of pain, broken dreams, and suffering contained in these ashes. It's interesting that the woman carried them with her all these years. Makes you wonder what else she's lugging around from her past."

He shook his head, his eyes filled with sadness. "Since you did your best to locate the mortuary's records, and because this is the will of the old man, I'd be honored to help. Not just because my favorite cousin asked me, but because this little girl deserves it. We don't even need to worry about a permit to scatter the ashes since there are precious few. Would ten o'clock on Saturday morning work for you? And will you be sure to get George Spell there if he's able and willing?"

Adrian smiled, nodded vigorously, then extended his fist across the table to bump Eddie's.

———

Adrian watched Eddie and George Spell at the end of the pier as they spread Baby Bridget's ashes on the water, just the two of them. It was an exquisite day. Early morning light was crystalline, striking small ripples on the lake and shattering into beautiful reflections. The air smelled of algae and newly mown grass. After they were finished, Eddie put his arm around the old man's shoulders and they spent some time quietly there, cocooned in the comfort provided by Eddie's presence.

As Adrian had expected, Eddie knew just how to arrange this small service. He had insisted on scattering the ashes alone with the old man. The number of those in attendance surprised Adrian and gave him a deep sense of satisfaction. Eddie had mustered over a dozen members from his church, most of them ex-gangbangers sporting sleeves of tattoos. Sylvia had also gotten a good response. Members from her support group, young and old, of all racial backgrounds, had turned out. Adrian estimated there were 30 people present to honor this child who had lived only ten days on planet Earth.

Eddie and George turned and walked back along the pier to the rest of the group, where the two of them took a place in the circle next to Adrian and Sylvia. Eddie called everyone into the moment, then began to share words of comfort and hope. He spoke of the significance of ashes as a reminder of the brevity of our lives. He recited words from Psalm 139, purportedly written by the ancient Israelite's King David: *For you created my inmost being; you knit me together in my mother's womb.*

Adrian had heard variations of these words from his cousin before, and he found his thoughts drifting. Adela's face came to mind—her smile, her lustrous dark eyes, the way she would cock her head slightly to the side when teasing him. Lately, she had said something that was still percolating in his soul. *Adrian, we've been together for years, but I feel like you hold yourself back from me at some level. How can I ever get to know you more fully?*

As he recalled her words, he thought of his father's remoteness, the box of Bridget's ashes, the sobbing of George in his living room, the old man's lament of *ten measly days*, the shotgun blast that had shattered the window of his Impala so long ago.

He came out of his reverie to find the group reciting the end of *The Lord's Prayer*, hearing those final transcendent words, *for thine is the kingdom and the power and the glory forever and ever. Amen.* Then, perhaps out of deference to the Twelve Step group present, Eddie led them all in the Serenity Prayer, an incantation that even Adrian, who never addressed God directly, found to be timeless, even eternal. He joined them, closing his eyes and bowing his head, and the word God seemed warm and necessary, stirring something inside him.

God, grant me the serenity to accept the things I cannot change, the courage to change the things I can, and the wisdom to know the difference. Amen.

As they closed, Eddie added, "Can we get an additional amen this morning for Baby Bridget?"

The group enthusiastically responded, and as that final affirmation rose into the morning sky, Adrian felt someone tapping his shoulder. He glanced to his left where Sylvia was motioning with her head to look behind them. He turned. Near the entrance to the park was a woman on a bike with a red backpack, her long silvery hair falling to her shoulders.

"Is it..." Adrian began to ask.

"Yes, yes," said Sylvia in a hushed voice.

Adrian turned to his right and whispered in George Spell's ear.

"Sir, I believe that's your daughter Carrie near the front gate."

George turned to look behind him and Adrian had

a clear view of the old man's eyes. At first they seemed startled, then filled with pain and longing. The whole group had turned now, and Adrian fully expected that Carrie would bicycle away. Instead, she began to slowly pedal towards them.

"My God, my God," said George, slowly opening his arms to embrace both his past and his future.

The Shaman

Those who do not want to lose their blindfolds for fear of the light, deserve the dark. – Quechan proverb

Cusco, Peru

"Not far now!" shouted my daughter, Jessie, from the front of the line.

Eight of us, a motley crew, were hiking along a train track. It took us twenty hours by bus to get there from Lima, leaning back and forth through endless switchbacks into the Andes. Now, just before sunset, the rails glinted in the fading light. The guy in front of me, a nomad from Australia, was merrily humming a tune I'd never heard, matching its cadence to his feet crunching the gravel. Further up the line, a couple from Arizona lit a joint, the funky sweetness wafting over our heads.

I inhaled the crisp mountain air and chuckled. Whenever I travelled with Jessie, it was bound to stretch my comfort zone. She's the freest spirit I've ever known, a world citizen, at home in whatever exotic locale she chooses. She had successfully monetized her escapades through YouTube and a podcast, calling them *Wander and Wonder,* so now she was unfettered, roaming at will, needing only her iPhone, laptop, and a Wi-Fi connection. And how can I describe the companions she draws to these treks? Bohemians? Naturalists? Alternative outliers? Take your pick, but I always find them enjoyable.

On that night, she was guiding us to the home of a modern-day shaman, a man named Jorge Vega she had discovered through her network. He had agreed to let her feature him for one of her online episodes.

Vega's story intrigued me, especially since I'm a professor at a liberal arts college. Educated at Harvard, he returned to his homeland of Peru to teach economics at the University of Lima. He had always aligned himself with leftist politics, but the crucible of the Peruvian Teacher's Strike in 2017 radicalized him further. He vehemently voiced his opposition to President Pedro Pablo Kuczynski's right-wing government and began to encourage activism among his students. The school's administration objected, then attempted to censor him, so he made a dramatic decision, resigning from academia to live among the poor in Cusco. There, he married a local woman, a community organizer in her own right, and the two of them worked tirelessly to strengthen farmers' collectives.

That portion of his life's arc was remarkable enough, but Vega had another incarnation. He had studied shamanic practices with a Quechan elder and now, alongside his organizing efforts, he offered spiritual guidance. From what Jessie had told me, it was an odd departure, something Vega's family and friends never expected.

Jessie planned to dig into all of it, and was thrilled that he would participate. She had been generating online buzz for a month. I asked to accompany her because I was curious to meet Vega, but also because a visit to Machu Picchu was on my bucket list.

I heard Jessie say "this way" as she led us onto a side street that ascended one of the hills surrounding the city. Cusco's economy thrives on tourism, but the money only spreads so far. A third of its residents live in poverty, and this *colonia* was visible proof. The dirt street was lined on both sides with humble adobe homes, most of them covered with chipped whitewash. The dwellings seemed half-finished, their roofs studded with rebar, as if this was a temporary settlement. Twilight grew deeper and I could hear chickens clucking from backyards as they prepared to roost.

Jessie paused at a red wooden door, barely visible, then turned to the rest of us. "Stay back a bit and let me speak to him. I wasn't sure how many of us there would be and I don't want to impose."

She knocked and the door opened promptly, interior light spilling onto the street. A thin man of medium height emerged. He had dark hair, a lean face, and was wearing simple slacks, shoes, and a black shirt. Wrapped around his shoulders was a colorful shawl, which I knew was called a *manta*. Woven into its rich alpaca fabric were totemic images of animals and geometric forms.

Jessie is fluent in Spanish, and I could hear them conversing. Vega turned and let his gaze sweep over our crew, his face lighting up with a smile.

"Bienvenidos," he called, gesturing for us to come inside. Then, in flawless English, "You are always welcome here."

———————

Vega's home had two rooms. The larger one contained a kitchen, sleeping area, and a dining table. The other was bare and unfurnished, with traditional blankets and sleeping pads piled along the walls. Overhead was a skylight, a break in the thatch and tile that covered the roof, and I could stars beginning to poke through the darkness. Vega told us we could use as much of the bedding as we wished for padding or extra warmth.

Dinner was delicious, and somehow, we were all able to fit around the table. Vega's wife, Killa—Quechan for moon—was short, thin, dressed in traditional garb, with bright eyes and a quick smile. She was also a skilled chef. Our fare was *pachamanca*, a traditional Andean dish of meat, vegetables, and local herbs, cooked underground in an earth oven. Its heady aroma filled the room, sluicing my salivary glands. Killa served it with a choice of strong Yerba Mate tea or *chicha de jora*, the fermented corn drink of Quechan culture.

For most of the meal, we engaged in small talk, but near the end, Vega asked for our attention.

"I understand that Jessie has given you the highlights of my story. If it is agreeable with all of you, will you take turns giving some background on who you are and where you come from? I would like to hear *your* stories."

Again, I was struck by his impeccable mastery of English, not surprising for a Harvard grad. He had an ease and charisma, holding court the way I imagined he had done countless times in his classrooms. His presence wrapped its arms around all of us. We readily nodded and began.

Noah, the young man from Australia, was taking a gap year to travel before medical school. After Peru, he planned to spend time in Patagonia.

The couple from Arizona—Michelle and Kevin— ran a string of successful Airbnbs in Sedona and Scottsdale, spending much of their time trekking the globe. They were ardent fans of Jessie's YouTube channel and podcasts.

Jen and Emily, two friends from Scotland, had hooked up with Jessie online. They were in their mid-20s, bubbly and gregarious, also on extended travels before the next chapters of their lives.

C.J. was more of an enigma. A man in his mid-40s, he had a dark beard, long curly hair, and the physique of a wrestler. During our entire trip, he had been preternaturally silent. When we attempted conversation, he was polite but left such huge gaps in responding that it was clear he preferred quietude. Now, he surprised us, telling how he had left his home in Massachusetts after his wife died prematurely, intent on traveling to some of the places they had always discussed. Machu Picchu was one of them.

Finally, it was my turn, so I gave the condensed version of my teaching career, my love for Jessie's mother, Ellen, and the ways that both of us stayed connected to the daughter that gave us such pride.

When I was finished, Vega asked, "Are you a Christian?"

The question was so out-of-the-blue, so abrupt, that I was taken aback, even a bit defensive.

"Why do you ask?"

Vega caught my tone and body language. "I don't mean to be rude. It's just that I did a little research before this visit and saw that the college where you teach has a Christian heritage."

I paused, trying to get in sync with his intent. "No," I finally said, "I'm not a Christian. The institution's roots are barely visible today. It's not required to profess any faith to teach there. If it had been, I would have gone elsewhere."

Vega nodded. "Again, I don't mean to be too bold. And I will not go into what Killa calls one of my tirades about how Christianity in the Americas has so often colluded with power structures and worsened oppression."

Killa cleared her throat and rolled her eyes. It made Vega laugh.

"My wife keeps me in check. What I'm more interested in is a passage from the Christian New Testament. Perhaps you know it. It's when Jesus says that he comes to us in the disguise of the hungry, the thirsty, the naked, the sick, and the imprisoned."

"I'm familiar with it," I said. "Why does it interest you?"

"Because I'm a student of not only the spiritual traditions of my own people, but of those around the world. I know that many revered Catholic saints had their conversion experiences because they believed they had encountered Christ in disguise. I think of St. Martin of Tours, who had a vision of Jesus coming to him as a naked beggar. Martin cleaved his cloak with a sword and gave half to the poor man. Later, in another dream, he saw Jesus wearing the half he had given away."

"That's true," I said, warming to our unexpected discourse, something I craved with my colleagues. "Do those stories speak to you?"

"They do, but not because I'm Christian. It has to do with my own tradition. Have you ever heard of *apus*?

"No."

"In Incan mythology, they are the spirits that live in these mountains. It's believed they have the power to shapeshift and appear in many forms—coyotes, pumas, condors, even as humans. Their intent is usually to teach a lesson."

I nodded and said nothing. I looked around the table, expecting that we were boring the others to tears, but they were listening intently.

"In 2016, I had the most lucid dream of my life," Vega continued. "A beggar came to me with an outstretched cup, asking for alms. His face was grizzled and he was dressed in rags. I reached into my pocket, withdrew a few coins, and gave them to him. He turned and started to walk away. Then he suddenly looked back at me, his face more youthful. He said in a very clear voice, 'What will you tell your students?'"

The memory was obviously emotional for Vega. He took a deep breath and settled back in his chair.

"That's trippy," said Noah. "Do you believe that was an *apu* visiting you?"

"I do," said Vegas, "and it changed me. Profoundly. People have always felt that what caused my departure from academia was my organizing and protesting for the teacher's strike. That was certainly part of it. But the seed planted in that dream by that *apu* is what ultimately drove me to be where I am this moment."

He looked down, as if the memory was still too powerful to fully absorb. His upper lip began to tremble. There was an awkward silence as we entered into his vulnerability.

"Kevin and I are firm believers that spirits communicate with us," said Michelle, as if to break the discomfort. "In the red rocks of Sedona, there are petroglyphs from the tribes that inhabited that area, and many of the images speak of the spirit world."

"In Scotland," said Jen, "there's the myth of the selkies who can shapeshift from seals to women."

"And they often appear," added Emily, "to lead people on a spiritual quest to Tír na nÓg, the other world."

Jorge lifted his face, looked around the circle, then lowered his head again. The intensity of his emotion was palpable in the room. Killa suddenly stood from her place at the table and walked behind her husband. She placed her hands gently on his shoulders and kissed the top of his head. I could hear her whispering something to him in Quechan. He gathered her arms around his shoulders like a comforting blanket.

———

C.J. may have been quiet during the day, but he was a world-class snorer at night. Even with earplugs, I could hear him rumbling. I couldn't understand why it didn't awaken the others.

I was restless for other reasons. Vega's story had moved me in unexpected ways. He didn't seem to have an agenda, but was simply sharing a life-changing epiphany, one that had forever altered the course of his life.

I thought about my teaching and the tenure I'd recently received. I thought about my students, most of them from middle to upper middle-class families that could afford the steep tuition. They were usually good pupils from solid families, but they were clearly sheltered from the harsher realities of our world. While other college campuses experienced protests for various causes, ours might see a random sign or two.

Sometimes I felt iconoclastic, with an urge to puncture all that complacency and status quo, but frankly, I feared the administration would label me a radical. The ethos at the university was to guide learners into their own conclusions, not to use our lecterns as pulpits. I mostly agreed with that philosophy, and I calmed my rebellious urges by downplaying my influence. *I'm just a middle-aged professor,* I said to myself. *Who will really listen to me?*

But I couldn't quell my concerns about what was happening in America. The rise of Christian Nationalism. A demagogue as a president, arrogantly crashing through guardrails that protect democracy. The widening gap between the haves and have nots. Brazen oligarchy. The growing intolerance for immigrants. Rising prejudice towards those with various gender identities. And, as Jessie always pointed out, the unsustainable consumption that fueled global warming.

It was enough to cause despair, but again, what could I really do? I thought of some verses from T.S. Eliot's "The Love Song of J. Alfred Prufrock."

> *I am no prophet—and here's no great matter;*
> *I have seen the moment of my greatness*
> *flicker,*
> *And I have seen the eternal Footman hold*
> *my coat and snicker,*
> *And in short, I was afraid.*

Vega wouldn't hear that snickering. His conviction to follow his own star made me feel an unexpected twinge of shame. It spoke of a passion and drive I hadn't known for years.

As I tossed and turned with these thoughts, breathing in the earthy smell of the room, I heard a flapping of powerful wings and saw a shape pass over the skylight. I looked up to see a huge bird perched on the roof, its head a fleshy pink, its beak curved like a talon. It peered down at me for a moment, then took off, dissolving into the night sky like disappearing ink. The noise had awakened others.

"Dad," whispered Jessie from her sleeping mat. "Was that a condor?"

"It sure looked like it."

"But what the hell would it be doing here at this hour?" said C.J. "Condors aren't nocturnal."

"Sort of creepy," whispered Kevin.

"Especially after what Vega shared at dinner," said Michelle.

Even under two warm blankets, I felt goosebumps rise on my skin.

In the morning, Jessie spent two hours with Vega recording his journey. When we left, thanking them profusely for their hospitality, both Killa and Jorge hugged us. When Jorge embraced me, he held me longer than I expected.

"*Tupananchiskama*," he whispered into my ear. "It means 'until next time,' because I sense we will meet again."

Then he released me and held my eyes for a few seconds with his intense gaze and smile.

"The pleasure was all mine," I whispered, my voice a bit hoarse.

We left and made our way to Poroy Train Station for our trip to Aguas Calientes, the city known as the portal to Machu Picchu. We had booked tickets to the site for the next day as well as hotel rooms that overlooked the Urubamba River, only a 20-minute walk to the entrance of the sacred ruins. Our plan was to get up before dawn and hike there to experience the sunrise.

We spent the afternoon in the city, taking photos for each other in front of the statue of Pachacuti, the Incan emperor who oversaw the building of Machu Picchu. We went from there to the bustling Mercado de Aguas Calientes with its maze of stalls selling native foods and handcrafts.

Since we all had different shopping agendas, we set a time to rendezvous back at the entrance, then went our separate ways.

The color and bustle of the market was intoxicating, especially the bright and intricate costumes of the women selling their wares. The air smelled of food dishes, fresh flowers, and the loamy aroma of potatoes, the staple of the Incan diet. I had never seen such a display of spuds—purple, green, yellow, red, orange, in a variety of shapes. I bought some dried coca leaves, chewing them the way locals do, letting the mild stimulant enhance my enjoyment of the scene. I sampled a couple empanadas and a tamale, washing them down with *chicha de jora*.

I was intent on finding a gift for Ellen, so when I saw a particular shawl, I knew it was perfect. I approached the older woman tending the stall. She was dressed in a *pollera* and *manta*, the traditional costume. My Spanish isn't great, but it's passable.

"Cuanto por esta manta?" I asked, pointing toward the prize I desired.

She looked up slowly with an amazing face bronzed by the sun and her lineage, her wrinkles speaking of vast experience. Her eyes were dark and penetrating, and they seemed to glint with an inner sense of humor. She gave me a price, we dickered a bit, and I handed her the money. She wrapped the *manta* in plain brown paper and presented it to me. I thanked her and began to walk away.

Then her voice called out to me from behind, **"Señor!"**

I turned around, wondering if I had shortchanged

her. Her eyes were now dead serious.

"What will you tell your students?" she asked, speaking crisp English, her voice completely different from how it had sounded moments before.

A shiver ran up my spine. "What?" I exclaimed.

She just nodded, looked down, and began arranging some of her wares.

I was still tingling when I joined the others at the entrance.

The next morning, we hiked to the entrance of Machu Picchu. I hadn't told anyone about my surreal experience in the *mercado*, not even Jessie. I was wondering if I had imagined it, a byproduct of chewing coca leaves and drinking corn beer. All I knew was that the moment—fictitious or real—was an extension of how Vega's story had affected me. I was clearly out of my depth, both emotionally and psychologically.

Let me tell you something. No matter how many travel videos you see about Machu Picchu, there is nothing like visiting in person. When we walked through the portal and I saw those iconic remnants against a backdrop of clouds and Andean peaks, it took my breath away. I felt like we were entering a mystical city in a mythical realm, the impression heightened by the gradual light of dawn spreading over the landscape—a slow, dramatic reveal.

Jessie reached over and took my hand. "Amazing, isn't it?"

"Even more beautiful than I imagined."

Then she took her hand, gently gripped my chin, and turned my face towards her. "Are you all right, Dad? You've been unusually quiet since our visit to the *mercado* yesterday."

She had a raging intuition. I shifted my eyes, a dead giveaway.

"Something happened that I don't even know how to explain. Just give me some space and I'll get there. In fact, I'd like to just walk around on my own, if that's okay."

She searched my eyes again—my delightful, intuitive daughter, an old soul if there ever was one. "Of course, Dad. Let me know if you want to talk."

She kissed me on the cheek, let go of my hand, and we separated to absorb the wonders of that place.

I wandered among the ruins, savoring the mountain air. I climbed to the Guardian House and asked another traveler to snap the classic postcard picture, something I had promised Ellen. Then I hiked back down and continued to walk aimlessly, enjoying the many llamas that graze unmolested among the stone structures.

Some of my friends speak of thin places where the supposed veil between this world and the next is more permeable. I had always scoffed at the notion, but I felt it now with an edge of vertigo.

I found a low wall and sat in the sunlight, surveying the vista as cloud shadows shifted over the landscape. My eyes were drawn to a family walking by. They had a girl with them adorned in traditional garb. A severe cleft palate twisted the lower part of her face. They were almost out of sight when the girl turned and locked her eyes on mine intentionally. She lifted her right hand and pointed at me, nodding her head.

I suddenly heard a powerful flapping of wings as a huge condor landed on the stone wall near me. Like the girl, it turned its flesh-covered head and stared right into me. I rubbed my eyes and called out to another group of tourists passing by.

"Do you see that?" I exclaimed.

"See what?" they asked with tolerant smiles.

I turned back, but the great bird was gone. In my ears, I heard Vega whisper, "*Tupananchiskama.*" I heard the Quechan woman ask, "What will you tell your students?"

I knew I would never be the same again, not in my perception of reality, or in how I would communicate to those in my classes. And at that moment, surrounded by the ruins of that timeless place, the thought filled me only with excitement.

Path of the Monarch

I sat on my usual park bench, perched by the pond with its fountain and water lilies. My therapist had told me, "Seek more serenity, Eric," so I was practicing a form of mindfulness, settling into the present, observing every nuance, color, and texture around me, gently dismissing extraneous thoughts. My brain is usually frantic, so it wasn't easy.

It was a pleasant day, the temperature in the mid-70s, and I could smell both the water and the fragrance of nearby cedar trees. I focused on the acrobatic dragonflies swooping over the pond, as if rehearsing for Cirque du Soleil. I have a friend who can name every species, but I was content to simply enjoy their grace and color as I slipped into a relaxed state of mind deeper than I'd ever known before.

That's when I saw the monarch butterfly. I wasn't surprised. It was their migration season, and the park had waystations that offered milkweed. This one, however, came closer than I expected, hovering near my face, inspecting me. Then it flew a few feet away, returned, and repeated its cycle three times, like it was urging me to follow. When it moved away again, I rose to my feet and did so with curiosity.

It stayed about ten feet ahead of me along a path that angled deeper into the park, a section left in a wild state for hikers. Its pace was brisk, so I had to hustle. We entered a dense grove of oaks, hackberries, and ashe junipers, and still the butterfly continued. When we came to what I knew was the furthest reach of the grounds—an area that abutted city neighborhoods—there were no homes visible. Just a beautiful meadow filled with prairie grass and wildflowers. The sky was a time-lapse video of shifting clouds against an azure sky.

This couldn't be. Was I daydreaming? I was about to turn around, but the monarch grew more insistent, coming closer again to get my attention, then gliding ahead. Despite the surrealism, I felt a sense of peace, and I could hear my therapist's voice say, "Just go with the flow, Eric."

I decided to follow, moving at a quicker pace. The butterfly and I seemed to sail through the meadow—bluebonnets, Indian paintbrush, and spider lilies flashing past—until the prairie surprisingly gave way to a desert filled with sandstone formations. In the distance was a jagged mountain peak.

By then, I was so committed that I didn't question the change of scenery or my resolve to let this vision unfold. The monarch led me past cliffs banded in red, yellow, and orange, until we came to a path leading up the mountainside.

This may have been an illusion, but my heavy breathing and the sweat on my forehead were very real.

Still, my guide insisted, drawing me up the trail, my leg muscles protesting. We climbed through a series of steep switchbacks until, rounding a corner, I saw someone sitting on a large stone, gazing down on the desert far below. He wore a bandanna around his head printed with images of kingly crowns.

When he turned and looked at me, it took my breath away.

Like most people, I've heard of doppelgangers, our supposed mirror counterparts. I've even read articles that said the phenomenon is real but statistically so rare that it's nearly impossible.

But there I was, staring at myself in the face.

"You're…" I stammered.

My doppelganger—let's call him D—simply laughed.

"I'm you? Yep. I've been waiting a long time to meet you, so I came up with the plan to send our friend here."

He motioned to the monarch who abruptly sailed down the cliffside and disappeared into the distance. I looked back at D, speechless. We stared at each other in silence for what felt like eternity.

Finally, I spoke. "Waiting? Why?"

D grinned. "Because you've been searching too long for answers. It's why you're seeing a therapist. It's why you've been meditating."

"And I suppose you have those answers?"

D laughed. "That sounds like something you'd say. Always outsourcing your power, always displacing your divinity."

I felt defensive, but given my long history of self-criticism, I shrugged it off.

"Look at me," said D. "Look at me the way you would look at yourself in the mirror."

I stared at him sitting in the sunlight. I saw the wrinkles that had formed on his forehead. In his eyes—*my eyes*—I saw a mix of sadness and resignation, and it pierced my heart.

"You see it, don't you?"

I nodded.

"Will you do something for me?"

I nodded again.

"Tell me—tell *yourself*—those lessons you know are true but seem unwilling to actualize."

The words came faster than I expected, as if an inner treasure chest burst open, every phrase springing into the light.

"Live in the present," I said. "Focus on the gifts of each day, rather than regrets or fears. Hold my loved ones close. Practice kindness towards everyone. Do the things that bring me joy. Remember that I will die and seize each day with gratitude."

D slid down from the rock and started towards me, stopping a few feet away. He started to clap. "Bravo! No more self-help books! No more gurus! Heaven is here. There is nowhere else. Heaven is now. There is no other time. And there's one more thing, grasshopper, one more piece of advice from yourself to you."

I felt stumped. No words came to mind.

"Let go," he said. "Let go, let go, let go, until it's as natural as breathing."

He placed his hands on my shoulders and moved so close that our noses were nearly touching.

"Practice with me," he said. "Each time we breathe out, whisper *let go*."

We tried it over and over, the two us inhaling, exhaling, and whispering together. Then D reached up and untied the bandanna covered with images of crowns and fastened it around my head. "We are the ruler of our thoughts," he said. "We are the monarchs of our mindfulness. Everything we need is inside us, all the eternal wisdom to live our lives to the fullest. This is the meaning of higher power, the force of creation living inside us and breathing with us. Loving us and desiring our freedom!"

Then suddenly he was gone, and I was on the bench again, the butterfly hovering a few feet away. I lifted my hand and it came to rest on my finger, slowly flapping its wings, like the rhythm of creation breathing in and out. Then it flitted away, joining the dragonflies in their dance over the pond.

I filled my lungs with oxygen and reached my hand to my head.

The bandanna with its crowns was still there.

The Last Dance

I would believe only in a God that knows how to dance. –
Friedrich Nietzsche

I'll never forget the first time I saw him.

    I was at my gym, furiously pumping an elliptical machine that faced a bank of treadmills. And there he was—a slight man, trim and fit, probably in his mid-70s, with the agility of someone much younger. He looked to be of Japanese ancestry, and he wasn't just exercising. He was dancing, literally, twirling with the grace and suppleness that someone from his generation might say was reminiscent of Fred Astaire, Gene Kelley, or Martha Graham. Sometimes he faced forward, sometimes backward, but he never missed a step in his pirouettes. It was mesmerizing. He didn't care what others thought, illustrating the famous meme: "Dance like there's nobody's watching."

    I'm usually reserved, even socially awkward, but

one day I worked up the courage to approach him as he completed his routine and stepped off the treadmill.

"Hello," I said, "my name's John. I just wanted to tell you that your moves are amazing! I love to see you work out. It gives me a sense of joy."

His eyes brightened and he nodded slightly. "My name's Hiroshi. Pleased to meet you, John, and thank you for your kind words."

That was it; end of conversation. But it wasn't the end of the enjoyment I got from watching him over the following year. Occasionally, he would acknowledge me with that graceful tilt of his head, but we never exchanged another word.

I knew I was being nosy, but one day I approached the manager of the gym, a gregarious guy who seemed to know the names and backgrounds of everyone. Some might say he's a gossip, but he definitely caters to his customers. He was at the front desk and greeted me with his usual salesperson smile.

I motioned my head towards Hiroshi. "That guy's phenomenal. Do you know anything about him?"

"He's pretty quiet," said the manager, "but I hear he owns that bicycle repair shop over on Broadway."

I'd driven by the place many times. It was called Pedal Pushers—small and quaint, with beautiful pictures of bicycles stenciled on the front glass. I'm not a biker, so I'd never been there, but it gave you a welcoming vibe.

"Interesting. I would have thought he ran a dance studio."

"I know, right?" said the manager. "He definitely

has some smooth moves."

That day, as I left the gym, I glanced back through its huge windows and saw him gyrating away. Our eyes met and he bowed his head in recognition.

———————

Weeks passed, then months. I saw Hiroshi less often, and finally he seemed to have vanished for good. I went to the oracle to get the scoop.

"I haven't seen Hiroshi for quite a while. Is he working out somewhere else?

"I don't think so," said the manager. "I heard through the grapevine that he was seriously ill. Cancer, I think. I even heard they have him in a hospice over in the Elm Street District."

At home that night, mulling it over, I decided to do something completely out of character. I resolved to visit the hospice. If Hiroshi had family, they might wonder why some guy would show up who had only exchanged a few words with their relative. But I didn't care. I felt compelled.

The next day after work, I drove to the small facility across town. Inside the lobby, a young woman sat at a reception desk. Soothing music poured from speakers mounted on the ceiling, and scented candles burned on a table. The air smelled faintly of lilac.

"May I help you?" she asked, her smile and gaze neutral.

"Yes, I believe you have a patient here named Hiroshi. I'm sorry. I don't know his last name."

"Are you a family member?"

"No. And I realize this might sound crazy since I only met him at our gym. I would just like to show him my support if possible."

The woman's eyes scoured me. She must have sensed my sincerity, because her face softened.

"He's in room 7. I've never noticed other visitors, so I don't see a problem with you looking in on him. I'm sure he'd appreciate it."

"Thank you," I said, then turned to walk down the hallway.

The door to his room was slightly ajar, so I gently pushed it open. He was alone, lying on the bed with his eyes closed. Already a diminutive man in life, he was a mere husk of himself as he neared death's portal.

When I got near, he opened his eyes and turned his head. Slowly, recognition spread over his face and he nodded slightly.

"John," he whispered.

"Yes, it's me."

He closed his lids and drifted away, his breathing labored. I pulled a chair next to the bed and, not knowing what else to do, took his hand in mine. We sat like that for many moments until he stirred.

"Help me get up," he whispered. "I've been lying here too long."

"I don't know. Maybe I should get a nurse."

He gripped my hand with unexpected strength. "No. Enough nurses and doctors. Just get me up. Please, John."

I helped him shift his feet over the side of the bed and lower them to the floor. He stood, shakily at first, leaning on my shoulder, but then, still holding my hand, he took a step, another one, and began to slowly twirl around like he was my dance partner. He did it again, then looked me in the eyes.

"Dance, John. Always dance."

And so, I did. Me, the wallflower at the prom. The guy who *always* felt awkward. The guy who held back from *ever* showing uncontrolled feelings to others.

As late afternoon sun filtered through the window of his room, Hiroshi and I danced in a way that felt as natural as running through a meadow or strolling through a garden at twilight. It filled my soul to overflowing.

———

I got busy, and though I intended to check in on Hiroshi, it was eight days before I returned to the hospice.

"I'm sorry," said the young woman at the desk. "He died a week ago. You got to see him just in time."

"Was there a service? Did I miss it?"

"No. A nephew of his from back east ordered cremation and the remains will be sent to some distant relatives in Japan. That's all I know."

"Can you at least tell me his last name?"

"Certainly. Yamato."

"I appreciate it," I said, turning to leave.

"Sir?" called the woman from behind me.

I turned. "Yes?"

"You seem like a good man. Thank you for brightening his last day on earth."

I felt a wave of emotion, so I just nodded, like he

did, to acknowledge her compliment.

At home that night, I searched the web and found one of the briefest obituaries I've ever read.

> Hiroshi Yamato, age 76, died peacefully on March 31, 2024. He was preceded in death by his wife Yukio of 43 years. The two of them owned Pedal Pushers, a popular bike shop in the community. If anyone wants to make a tribute, Hiroshi asked that you support Dance Without Limits, a nonprofit that provides dance therapy to individuals with disabilities.

I found the organization's website and made a sizable donation in his honor. Then I turned off my computer and went to the window. I live in a second-floor condo that overlooks a city park with a pond and hiking trails. It was near sunset, a golden glow suffusing the scene. I saw a family walking along the water's edge, their young boy skipping ahead of them with that joy we too often lose in adulthood.

"Keep dancing, boy," I whispered. "Always dance."